GW00504166

GINETTE CHEVALLIER

spent her childhood in France, moving to Paris at the age of eighteen to become a model for some of the most famous couturiers. She has also worked as a photographic model and an antiques dealer and now divides her time between Monaco and London where she runs a very popular Radio London phone-in on practical hints.

by the same author

1000 THINGS YOU OUGHT TO KNOW

STAINS & FABRICS

1,000 THINGS
you ought to know

GINETTE CHEVALLIER

Illustrated by Malcolm Bird

BANTAM PRESS

NEW YORK · LONDON · TORONTO · SYDNEY · AUCKLAND

TRANSWORLD PUBLISHERS LTD
61−63 Uxbridge Road
London W5 5SA

TRANSWORLD PUBLISHERS (AUSTRALIA) PTY LTD
26 Harley Crescent Condell Park NSW 2200

TRANSWORLD PUBLISHERS (NZ) LTD
Cnr Moselle & Waipareira Aves
Henderson Auckland

Published 1986 by Bantam Press, a division of
Transworld Publishers Ltd
Copyright © U.D.F. 1986
Illustrations copyright © Malcolm Bird 1986

British Library Cataloguing in Publication Data

Chevallier, Ginette
Stains and fabrics: 1,000 things you ought to know.
1. Spotting (Cleaning)
I. Title
648'.1 TP932.6

ISBN 0-593-01022-1

Printed in Great Britain by
Hazell Watson & Viney Limited, Aylesbury

I dedicate this book to my mother and . . . to all of you 'spotty dicks' out there!

Contents

Preface   10

Cleaning Agents   11
Care of Fabrics   23
Stains   47
Miscellaneous   119

Index   127

Preface

I wrote this book because I am a little particular about cleanliness — although not as bad as my mother. Every Sunday morning when we were children, my brother and myself, dressed in our Sunday best, would stand to attention in our room waiting for Mother's weekly inspection. She would examine us from head to toe and our room from top to bottom — and woe betide us if she ever found a 'spot' because we would get a lecture on cleanliness and be made to get rid of it straight away. Somehow I always seemed to be the one doing the cleaning — my brother very cleverly bribed me for my services!

As I say, I am *not* as bad as my mother . . . but I'm getting there — maybe it's hereditary! All I can say is that I find it more than annoying to see an impeccably dressed man wearing a stained tie, when I know that a little piece of bread or some talcum powder would do the trick and make the stain disappear! And if I see a white water-ring on my hostess's beautiful wooden table, my fingers itch to rub cigarette ash into it and restore it to its former beauty.

It's all here in *Stains and Fabrics: 1,000 Things You Ought to Know*! It will be, dear readers, our little contribution to the world, making it a cleaner place to live in.

NB: for the purposes of this book I have used the very approximate measure of 2 pints to 1 litre.

CLEANING AGENTS

Acetic acid

A colourless liquid which neutralizes any alkali effects on fabrics. (Alkaline residue comes from hard-water calcium soap deposits and takes the brightness out of colour.) Dilute 2 teaspoons of acetic acid with 2 pints/1 litre of water for the last rinse. As a stain-remover, dilute 1 teaspoon of acetic acid to 10 teaspoons of water. If the dye changes colour when using acetic acid, sponge the fabric with ammonia. Vinegar is a form of acetic acid and a good substitute for it.

From chemists

Acetone

A highly flammable solvent. Good to remove nail varnish, paint and oils (animal and vegetable). *Do not use* on acetate fabrics.

From chemists

Alcohol

Organic chemicals, methylated spirit and surgical spirit are

13

forms of ordinary rubbing alcohol. These solvents are good for removing stains on fabrics. First test if dyes are affected by the alcohol. Dilute the alcohol in two parts of water for man-made fabrics.

From chemists and hardware shops

Alkalis
As opposed to acids (ammonia, washing soda and other soda compounds). They neutralize acids and change colours in some dyes.

Ammonia
Alkali and grease solvent. Gives off strong fumes, so use in a well-ventilated room and wear rubber gloves to avoid skin contact. Keep in a cool, dark place. Buy cloudy household ammonia as it has a little soap added to it. It removes stains such as grass, chocolate and blood from fabrics. For household purposes use a solution of 1 part ammonia to 10 parts water. *Do not use* ammonia and bleach together; the combination releases a dangerous gas.

From hardware shops

Amyl acetate
Useful solvent to remove stains such as lacquers, cellulose paint, nail varnish, etc. It is poisonous and flammable. It can be used on fabrics that cannot be treated with acetone.

From chemists

Benzine
Inflammable liquid, distilled from crude petroleum. Used as a solvent and in dry-cleaning.

From chemists

Bicarbonate of soda (baking soda)
Useful for removing stains from fabrics, cleaning chrome, paint, ovens, china, glass, refrigerators. Cleans teeth. Softens water. Appeases tummy aches. Cleans jewellery, etc., etc. It is a *must* in the house.

From chemists and supermarkets

Bleach (household bleach)
Useful to bleach white cotton and linen. Soak in a mild bleach solution (1 tablespoon to 2 pints/1 litre water) for ten minutes, rinse thoroughly. *Do not use it* on wool or silk. Bleach can be used as a lavatory cleaner, but *do not* mix it with vinegar, ammonia or any other household products; it will produce a highly irritating gas which can cause serious injury. Bleach can lose its effectiveness if stored for too long.

From hardware shops and supermarkets

Blue/washing blue
Makes white look whiter.

From supermarkets

Borax (laundry and domestic)
It is a compound of mineral salt, which is a combination of boracic acid and soda. It loosens grease and dirt, and is also an antiseptic. Some old stains on fabrics, such as jam, ice cream, coffee, etc., will loosen off if just soaked in a borax solution (1 tablespoon to 1 pint/$\frac{1}{2}$ litre of warm water).

From chemists and supermarkets

Bran
The husk of grain sifted from the flour, after grinding. Used hot or warm as an absorbent to clean velvet upholstery, felt hats and furs.

From chemists and health food shops

Castor oil
Obtained from the seeds of the castor oil plant. A very good leather-conditioner. First clean the leather; next with a soft cloth apply a small amount of oil, rub it well into the leather and wipe off the excess.

From chemists

Chlorine bleach
See under *Bleach*.

Chlorine lime
A combination of lime and chlorine gas. A good disinfectant for outside dustbins and damp basements.

From hardware shops

Detergents (synthetic detergents)
Made from petroleum, natural fats and oils, used to clean around the house and for dish-washing and laundry. Available in liquids and powders. Laundry detergents are of two types: light-duty for delicate fabrics and heavy-duty biological (enzyme) detergents for more heavily soiled fabrics. Always follow the instructions on the packet. Liquid detergent is a very good stain-remover.

From supermarkets

Emery cloth/sandpaper
Use as an abrasive to polish metal, hard stones and wood. It can be bought in varying degrees of roughness graded from coarse to fine.

From hardware shops

Enzymes
See *Detergents*.

Ether
Dissolves animal fats and oils. A powerful anaesthetic liquid. Use carefully, in a well-ventilated room.

From chemists

Eucalyptus oil
A volatile, aromatic, straw-coloured oil. It will remove grease stains on any fabric, even the most delicate, without leaving a trace. Also used in medicine as an inhalant.

From chemists

French chalk
Powdered, a kind of talc. Tailors use it to mark cloth; often used as an absolvent on fresh grease stains on fabrics, wood,

paper, etc. It is completely harmless and does not leave a ring.
From chemists

Fuller's earth
It is composed of a variety of clays and is used as an absolvent to remove grease and oil stains from non-washable fabrics (suede, fur, tapestry, etc.).
From chemists

Gilder's white
See *Whiting*.

Glycerine
A colourless, odourless liquid which is a useful solvent to loosen many kinds of stain on fabrics. Use neat or as a solution with equal quantities of warm water, following instructions.
From chemists

Hydrogen peroxide (20 vol.)
A colourless liquid. Buy it in 20 volume strength. Keep it in a cool, dark place. It is used for delicate treatments, such as cleaning marble and ivory and removing light scorch marks or stains such as blood, ink, perfume, etc., from fabrics. *Do not use* on pure nylon. Hydrogen peroxide will work better if kept in the refrigerator.
From chemists

Iodine
A volatile chemical element used as an antiseptic in medicine and also used in photography. It is also used to remove silver nitrate stains.
From chemists

Jeweller's rouge
An abrasive red powder, used as a paste with methylated spirit or water for cleaning and polishing glass, jewellery, silver, etc.
From hardware shops

Kerosene

A volatile oil. Highly flammable. Kerosene is used to remove rust on metals, and stains on vinyl upholstery.

From hardware shops

Lanolin

A waxy yellow substance which is obtained from wool grease. Used in cosmetics, and can also be used as a leather-conditioner.

From chemists

Linseed oil

Comes from the common flax seeds. Highly flammable. Used in oil paints, varnishes and furniture polishes. It can be bought 'raw' or 'boiled'. Boiled linseed oil can be used to darken wood and to rub off water marks on furniture (mixed with equal proportions of turpentine or mixed to a paste with cigar or cigarette ash).

From chemists and hardware shops

Methylated spirit

A volatile and inflammable liquid. It should be handled with care. A grease solvent, good for cleaning mirrors, glass, jewellery, ivory, and for removing grease stains from fabrics. It will also remove ballpoint or felt-tip ink stains, chocolate, coffee or mud stains from non-washable fabrics. For man-made fabrics, dilute 1 part methylated spirit to 2 parts of water. *Do not use* on french-polished wood surfaces; it will dissolve the polish.

From chemists and hardware shops

Oxalic acid

Used as a bleach or a stain-remover (ink, rust). Always wear gloves when using oxalic acid, dissolve in warm water (1 tablespoon of oxalic acid crystals to 1 pint/ $\frac{1}{2}$ litre of warm water), in a glass container as it may damage a metal one. Poisonous. Keep in a safe place and labelled.

From chemists

Paraffins

Colourless, odourless, useful as a solvent for grease. Paraffin wax can be used as a substitute for beeswax. Paraffin oil is poisonous and is used to get rid of rust on metal. From ironmongers or petrol stations.

Liquid paraffin is not poisonous and is used as a laxative. It is also a good substitute for face cream. From chemists.

Paris white

See *Whiting*.

Peroxide

See *Hydrogen peroxide*.

Petroleum jelly

See *Vaseline*.

Pumice

A piece of lava useful for smoothing rough skin.

Powdered pumice is used as an abrasive; it is a good polisher and scourer. Many commercial scouring powders include pumice powder.

From chemists and hardware shops

Rottenstone

A soft stone used for polishing metals. Powdered rottenstone mixed with linseed oil will remove white spots from furniture. Apply lightly with a soft cloth. Follow the grain of the wood.

From hardware shops

Rouge

See *Jeweller's rouge*.

Saddle soap

A special soap for cleaning leather. Good on all polished leather.

From hardware shops

Sandpaper
See *Emery cloth*.

Silver sand
A clean, very fine sand, used as an abrasive and absolvent.

From ironmongers and domestic stores

Solvent
A liquid used to dissolve grease stains from fabric and other materials. Water, acetone, ammonia, amyl acetate, glycerine, methylated, surgical and white spirits, paraffin and turpentine are all solvents.

Spanish white
See *Whiting*.

Surgical spirit
Used as a solvent to remove grease stains on fabric. Flammable.

From chemists

Teak oil
Used on teak wood to clean and polish.

From ironmongers

Turpentine
Used as a solvent for varnish, wax, paint, etc. Flammable. It is quite expensive. White spirit will sometimes be as effective and is much cheaper.

From chemists

Vaseline (petroleum jelly)
A soft greasy substance, used as a soothing ointment. It is also used to loosen heavy grease and tar stains on fabric, before using a solvent. Used also on metal as a rust preventative and for conditioning leather.

From chemists

Vinegar

White vinegar is a mild acid and a most useful cleaning agent around the house. Few other products have as many culinary and chemical virtues. It dissolves dirt deposits, diminishes scum and film from soap, and softens water. It is used in stain removal to counteract alkalis and to restore colours altered by them. Hot vinegar will soften paint-brushes.

Washing soda

This is a very strong concentrated alkali, and can be injurious to the skin, so wear rubber gloves when using it. It cleans grease from waste-pipes, is used for cleaning silver and copper, and softens water for cleaning purposes.

From some domestic stores, chemists and ironmongers

White spirit

A good turpentine substitute. It is used as a solvent or thinner for paint. It removes grease and stains from fabric and leather. Dilute in 2 parts of water for man-made fibres. Flammable and toxic.

From chemists and hardware shops

Whiting

A fine powdered chalk, used as an abrasive. Whiting is known by different names, depending on how fine and free from grit it is. The Spanish white and the gilder's white are used to polish silver; Paris white is the finest of the whiting powders.

From hardware shops

CARE OF FABRICS

General hints

Bleach
The damage caused by a small spill of bleach on fabric can be greatly diminished if the spill is immediately impregnated with hydrogen peroxide (20 vol.). Leave for one minute before rinsing well.

To get the smell of bleach out of linen, add a small quantity (1 teaspoon to 1 pint/ $\frac{1}{2}$ litre) of distilled malt vinegar to the last rinse. Always dilute the bleach in cold water, for if hot water is used it will act too quickly and may ruin the fabric. It is better to soak the fabric in a weaker solution for longer.

Colour fastness
Test your clothes for colour fastness before washing with other items for the first time. Dampen a small area with water and press it between two pieces of white cloth. If the white cloth gets stained with the colour, the item should be washed separately.

When washing coloured fabrics add half a teacup of salt to the water to prevent the colour from running.

Creases

Creases in clothes can be removed if dampened with vinegar and pressed with an iron.

Dry-cleaning

These symbols tell your cleaner which dry-cleaning agents are suitable.

 Do not dry-clean

 Do not machine-wash

 Do not wash at all

Dyeing

To dye a garment black successfully, use an equal quantity of navy blue dye with the black dye. This will prevent the fabric taking on a greenish tinge.

Frosty washing

To prevent linen or clothes getting frosty on the line in the winter, add half a teacup of salt to the last rinse.

Ironing

You will get better and quicker results when ironing if you put a strip of aluminium foil the length of the ironing-board underneath the padded cover. The foil will become hot and your clothes will be heated from both above and below.

If you have to stop ironing before you have ironed all the articles you have dampened, keep the remainder in a plastic bag until you are ready to press them. Don't leave them damp for too long.

Ironing symbols on garments

Cool iron	For acrylics, triacetate, polyester, nylon and silk
Warm iron	For wool, wool and nylon mixtures, polyester and cotton mixtures
Hot iron	For cotton, linen, viscose
Do not iron	

Irons

To remove starch sticking to the iron, or to remove the sticky patch left after scorching a fabric, sprinkle a piece of paper with fine kitchen salt and rub the iron backwards and forwards over it until the base becomes smooth again. You can also rub the iron with half a lemon dipped in fine kitchen salt.

Residues of burnt man-made fibre left on the iron can be removed by first bringing the temperature of the iron to very hot and scraping as much of the residue off as possible with a wooden spatula. Next let the iron cool and finish with a fine steel-wool pad.

Steam irons can get furred unless you use distilled water (from the chemist) or water which has been boiled for half an hour and left to cool so that the chalk settles at the bottom.

To remove fur, half-fill the iron with vinegar. Warm the iron and press the steam button until all the vinegar has evaporated, then fill the iron with distilled or boiled water and steam it out again until the iron is dry. The iron will be clean inside and ready to be used again.

A few drops of your favourite toilet water mixed with the water inside your steam iron will perfume your linen delicately; or, if you don't have a steam iron, spray your ironing-board when you are pressing.

Tea towels/handkerchiefs

Press three or four at a time by placing them one on top of the other, then press the top and bottom one.

Tea towels will not leave fluff on drinking-glasses if a little starch is added to the final rinse when washing them.

Textile care
Labelling Code

	Machine	Hand	
[1/95]	Very hot	Hand-hot 50°C/120°F	White linen and cotton without special finishes
[2/60]	Hot	Hand-hot 50°C/120°F	Colourfast linen and cotton without special finishes
[3/60]	Hot	Hand-hot 50°C/120°F	White nylon, white polyester and cotton mixtures
[4/50]	Hand-hot	Hand-hot 50°C/120°F	Coloured nylon; polyester; acrylic and cotton mixtures; cotton rayon with special finishes; coloured polyester and cotton mixtures
[5/40]	Warm	Warm 40°C/100°F	Non-colourfast linen, cotton or rayon
[6/40]	Warm	Warm 40°C/100°F	Acrylics; acetates; blends of these fabrics with wool; mixtures of wool and polyester
[7/40]	Warm	Warm 40°C/100°F	Wool; silk; wool mixtures with cotton or rayon
[8/30]	Cool	Cool 30°C/85°F	Silk; acetate fabrics with colours not fast at higher temperatures
[9/95]	Very hot	Hand-hot 50°C/120°F	Cotton can be boiled but requires drip-drying

Individual fabrics

Acetate
Silk-like fabric. Wash by hand in warm soapy water; do not spin unless mentioned on label and do not wring as tiny creases will appear in the fabric. Get rid of excess water by rolling in a towel or leaving to drip-dry. Press while damp with a warm iron.

For knitwear the last rinse should be cold; the cold water cools the fibres so that the garment will not crease when wrung out or spun.

Acrylic (Acrilan, Courtelle, Orlon, Dralon, nylon)
Acrylic knitwear: to get rid of the little fluffy balls forming on the knitwear, brush the dry garment with a hard nylon brush — or shave it with an electric razor. Always rinse an acrylic garment in cold water; the cold water cools the fibres so that the garment will not crease when wrung out or spun. Before ironing, do not sprinkle water on an acrylic garment which has dried out because the water will not be evenly spread and it will leave marks. Wet the entire garment and press with a cool iron.

Do not forget that acrylic fabrics do not dye successfully.

Angora

Fabric made from the wool of an Asiatic goat; also made with the fine hair of a white rabbit with pink eyes. Wash as for wool – use lukewarm water and special wool detergents. Handle gently. Rinse in lukewarm water. Roll in a towel to absorb excess water, then shake the garment out gently to fluff the yarn up, before shaping and putting it flat to dry.

If angora knitwear loses its hair, put it in a plastic bag in the refrigerator for a few days.

Batiste

A very light fabric made of cotton or linen, so it must be washed accordingly. Follow instructions for *Cotton* or *Linen*.

Brocade

Heavy silk or velvet fabric threaded with silver or gold thread, often raised with designs of flowers, leaves, etc. It should be dry-cleaned. Press the material on the wrong side with a warm (not hot) iron over a piece of thin cloth.

A little dry powdered magnesia rubbed on and left for an hour or two will also clean lamé fabric. Brush away the powder with a soft brush.

Gold or silver lamé fabric can be kept shiny if it is regularly rubbed gently with a chamois skin. If the fabric is dull-looking, rub with a very warm piece of crustless bread. Repeat the operation until the lamé shines again, or rub the fabric with warm bran and then finish shining with the chamois skin.

Calico

Made from fine cotton. Follow instructions for *Cotton*.

Candlewick

Bedspreads and dressing-gowns are sometimes made of candlewick. It may be pure cotton or cotton mixed with synthetics (see label). Clean according to the type of fabric. Shake well after washing and when dry shake again to fluff up the pile.

Canvas
Wash in warm water and detergent. Scrub with a brush if very dirty. Rinse well.

Cashmere
Made from soft hair of certain goats. Cashmere fabric must be dry-cleaned. Wash cashmere sweaters very carefully following instructions for *Wool*, using the finest wool detergent.

Cheesecloth
A very light, loosely woven cotton fabric. It should be hand-washed to keep its shape. Do not wring. Roll in a towel to absorb excess water. Iron while damp. Put back into shape while ironing.

Chenille
Clean according to the type of fabric, for the material could have been made from silk or be a synthetic (see label). Shake from time to time while drying to fluff the pile. When dry brush up the tufts gently with a dry, clean, soft brush. Do not iron.

Chiffon
Very soft, gauze-like fabric made of silk or synthetic (viscose) fibres (see label). Clean according to the type of fabric. Dresses or blouses should be dry-cleaned.

Flimsy chiffon or similar materials should be placed in a jar with warm water and some borax. Screw the top on and shake the jar to clean the chiffon without rubbing. Rinse in clear water and pat it dry with a towel. Avoid ironing when it is too wet or it will stiffen. Do not sprinkle dry chiffon with water to dampen as the spots will mark.

Chintz
Cotton cloth printed in colourful designs with a glazed finish on the right side. If the glaze wears off after many washes, it can be restored professionally. Old chintz should be dry-cleaned. New chintz can be washed very carefully in lukewarm water with a mild detergent. Do not rub or twist. Rinse in lukewarm

31

water and then give a final rinse in cold water. Pat it in a towel to absorb excess water. Iron while still damp.

To prevent fading when washing chintz, wash it in bran water instead of soapy water. Dry in the shade and iron while still damp.

(To make bran water, use 1 teacup of bran to 6 pints/3 litres of water; bring to the boil and simmer for half an hour, then strain and throw away the bran. When bran water is used no detergent is necessary. Bran water is perfect for washing delicate fabrics; i.e., chintzes, muslins, etc.)

Corduroy
Made from cotton, a hard-wearing velvety fabric, completely washable. For the best results wash by hand. Do not wring or twist. Shake well, smooth the pile in the right direction while still damp. Iron on the wrong side while still damp.

Cotton
A cloth woven from cotton threads can be washed in very hot water. White cotton can be boiled to make it whiter. Wash coloured and white materials separately. Most colourfast cottons will stand hot water but they might bleed slightly for the first two or three washes. Some cottons will shrink when washed for the first time. Most cottons can be ironed with a hot iron. Starching cotton will help keep it clean longer and make it look crisper.

Cotton sometimes gets yellowed by chlorine bleach. To make it look snow white again soak the cotton for a few hours in a solution of white vinegar (1 part) and cold water (8 parts).

Half a teacup of beer added to the last rinse will cheer up your black cotton garment and make it look like new.

Crêpe, and crêpe-de-chine
Crêpe is a thin cloth with a wrinkled surface. To clean follow the label instructions. If it is washable, wash by hand in warm

soapy water. Rinse well and iron on the wrong side, while still damp.

Crêpe-de-chine is a lighter fabric made of silk or synthetic fibres. Clean according to the type of fabric. Iron on the wrong side while still damp.

Some crêpe fabrics shrink after washing. To get it back to normal press it very wet.

Dacron
See Synthetic fabrics.

Damask
Reversible fabric made of linen, silk or synthetic fibres (see label). Shiny threads are woven into the fabric to make wavy designs. Clean according to the type of fabric.

Denim
Denim is usually made of cotton. Wash on its own as the colour never becomes fast. Press while still damp.

Felt

A matted fabric made out of compressed fur, hair or wool. It cannot be washed as it would shrink terribly. Dry-clean.

To clean felt make a paste with french chalk and white spirit. Lightly rub it into the felt. Leave to dry, then brush it out.

Use hot bran to clean felt. Heat the bran in the oven and then rub over the felt; it will absorb any grease. Brush thoroughly.

White felt can be cleaned by rubbing powdered magnesia into the felt with a clean cloth. Leave the powder on for twelve hours, then shake off the excess and brush with a clean stiff brush.

To clean white felt make a paste with some arrowroot and cold water. With your fingers, carefully coat the felt with the paste and allow it to dry thoroughly before brushing it off.

Marks on light felt can be dealt with sometimes by gently rubbing with fine clean sandpaper.

Fine lingerie

Do not wring out your lingerie after washing; get the excess water out by putting it in your salad spinner!

Flannel

A loosely woven woollen fabric. It should be dry-cleaned for best results. Small items can be washed by hand following instructions for *Wool*.

Gaberdine

A finely ribbed woollen fabric. It should only be dry-cleaned.

Hessian

A coarse sackcloth made from natural fibres. Should be dry-cleaned.

Jersey

Fine woollen jersey should be dry-cleaned. The viscose version should also be dry-cleaned.

Other synthetic jerseys can be washed following the label instructions. Do not twist. Roll in a towel to absorb excess water. Can also be lightly spun.

Lace

Old delicate lace should be placed inside a pillowcase to be washed. Place the pillowcase in warm soapy water, press gently, do not wring or squeeze. Rinse carefully and iron the lace under a cloth in order not to catch it and tear it. Synthetic lace should be washed and pressed following the instructions for the type of fibre it is made of.

To clean delicate old lace, spread it on a piece of white blotting-paper. In a saucepan gently heat some potato flour until quite hot and then spread a thick layer of the hot flour over the lace, pressing it down with your fingers. Leave until cool and then remove with a soft brush. Repeat the operation if necessary.

To clean very delicate black lace fold the lace to a square and place it inside a container. Cover it with beer and leave to soak for twenty minutes. Knead the square of lace with your fingers without rubbing. Rinse in lukewarm water.

To dye white lace, dip the lace in a saucepan filled with a weak strained brew of tea or coffee. Simmer, stirring, until the desired colour is obtained.

New laces can become antique-looking if dipped in tea or an infusion of camomile for a lighter tone. Black laces look better after a bath in sweetened black coffee. Then press between two clean pieces of cloth.

Keep old lace in a dry, warm place, airing it from time to time, if not in use often. Black lace has a tendency to mould if not aired.

Lace veil

To rejuvenate a lace veil lay it flat on a towel and sprinkle with one of the following: talcum powder, french chalk, powdered magnesia, bicarbonate of soda, or powder starch. Rub it into the fabric with your fingers and leave it for two hours, then shake well to remove all traces of powder.

If the veil is not too delicate, use the same products as above but place the veil in a plastic bag with the powder and shake.

Spraying the veil with a dry shampoo is also a very efficient method of cleaning.

Linen

A fine cloth made from flax. Treat as cotton. Iron on the wrong side with a hot iron when still very damp. Creases in dry linen are practically impossible to get rid of.

New linen is sometimes very stiff; to get rid of the stiffness, soak the material in warm water to which a few soda crystals and some salt have been added.

Mohair

A fabric made from the Angora goat. Follow label instructions. After many washes mohair woollens have a tendency to fur.

Moiré

Made of silk or synthetic fibres moiré has an appearance like the surface of water. It should be dry-cleaned only.

Muslin

Very fine, thin cotton fabric with large open weave. Hand-wash only as for cheesecloth.

Net

Most net curtains are now made of synthetic fabrics. Do not machine-wash them; the treatment is too harsh. Do not wring. Instead fill up one-third of your bathtub with lukewarm water, add two teacups of ammonia and mix well. Take your net curtains, shake out the dust, fold them lengthwise, then across, and lay them in the bathtub keeping them underwater. Leave to soak for half an hour. Next run out the dirty water without moving the net curtains and replace with lukewarm water. Add some synthetic detergent and squeeze the water through the material, but do not rub or twist. Leave to soak for ten minutes. Rinse several times by running out the dirty water and replacing it with lukewarm water, without moving the folded net curtains.

After the last rinse, lift the folded net curtains out of the water and hang them on a rack placed across the bathtub. Leave to dry for half an hour before laying them folded on a towel. Roll them up lightly to absorb moisture and hang them at the window where they will finish drying. This way the net curtains do not need ironing. If you have to iron them, do it when they are still damp, with the iron on synthetic setting.

Nylon

To prevent white nylon from becoming yellow, soak it first in a strong solution of warm water and bicarbonate of soda. Leave to soak for at least two hours.

See *Synthetic fabrics*.

Oilcloth

A cotton material made waterproof with oil. Clean by wiping with a damp cloth. Do not fold when wet as it would crack at the corners. Acetone and alcohol are very damaging to its shiny surface.

To make oilcloth as new again, lightly beat the white of an egg and rub it over the oilcloth with a soft cloth. Leave it to dry and then polish with a dry cloth. Pure vinegar will also bring back colours to an oilcloth.

To remove marks left by hot plates, rub the marks with a cloth dipped in camphor oil.

Organdie

Transparent cotton muslin. Hand-wash gently in warm soapy water. Do not wring. Roll in a towel to absorb moisture and iron while still damp. After many washings organdie might need to be slightly starched.

For embroidered organdie iron on the wrong side.

Organza

Dress material made of various fibres — nylon, silk, rayon, etc. Dry-clean or wash according to the type of fabric. Follow label instructions.

Orlon

See *Synthetic fabrics*.

Piqué

A ribbed cotton fabric. Wash like any cotton fabric. Iron on the wrong side.

Polyester

A man-made fibre. It dries quickly and normally requires no ironing; but, if a little ironing should be needed, use a cool iron on the dry fabric.

See under *Synthetic fabrics* for washing instructions.

Poplin
Can be made of cotton or synthetic fibres. Wash accordingly.

Rayon
A silk-like man-made fibre. Can be hand-washed or dry-cleaned following label instructions. When in doubt about washing follow the directions for *Acetate*.

Satin
Glossy fabric made of silk or synthetic fibres. Clean accordingly.

A delicate fabric to wash — add a little sugar and some vinegar to the last rinse. Always press damp.

Serge
Strong twilled woollen fabric made from pure wool mixed with cotton or synthetic fabric. Dry-clean.

Shantung
A coarse silk fabric. It is also made of synthetic fibres nowadays. Wash according to the fibre it is made of.

Silk
To distinguish pure silk from artificial silk pull a few threads from the fabric, double it and roll it between your fingers to make a double thread of two to three inches (approximately 8 cm). Take a match and light one end of the thread. If the thread burns a little, then dies out forming a small ball of charcoal, it is pure silk. If the thread burns easily in one go to the end, it is not pure silk.

A lustrous soft fabric, which should be dry-cleaned. If the silk is washable, handle with care using a mild synthetic detergent in lukewarm water. Do not rub or wring.

Add a little vinegar and sugar to the last rinse. Roll in a towel to absorb moisture.

Iron on the wrong side while still damp. If allowed to dry, wet it again entirely and roll it in a towel to absorb moisture. Slight dampening would cause water marks.

Another way is to let the silk dry completely and then place it in a plastic bag to which 3–4 tablespoons of water have been added. Close the bag and leave overnight. In the morning you will find the silk evenly damp and ready to be pressed.

White silk which has become yellowish with age can be brought back to its original whiteness if soaked in a bath of water, hydrogen peroxide and ammonia (2 pints/1 litre of water to $\frac{1}{4}$ pint/125 ml hydrogen peroxide and one tablespoon of ammonia). Check the progress from time to time.

To renovate black silk, slice some raw potatoes and pour boiling water over them. When cold, sponge the right side of the silk with this liquid and iron on the wrong side. Stale beer is also good.

Another method of renovating silk is to sponge it with a weak solution of household ammonia and water (2 tablespoons ammonia to 1 pint/ $\frac{1}{2}$ litre cold water) and press it on the wrong side.

A shine on silk will disappear if rubbed along the weave of the material (not across) with a solution of one teaspoon of borax to a teacup of water.

Scorch marks on silk can be removed by applying a paste made of bicarbonate of soda and water to the mark. Leave to stand for at least two hours. Next brush off the bicarbonate of soda, stretch the affected part over a basin and pour cold water over it a few times.

Raw silk should be dry-cleaned.

Pongee soft unbleached silk: To wash follow instructions for silk above. Do not iron pongee too wet or it will stiffen.

Suede
Natural untreated leather should only be dry-cleaned. It can sometimes be washed by hand in soapflakes following label instructions.

Synthetic fabrics (Dacron, nylon, Orlon, polyester)
Man-made fibres. If instructions are given by the manufacturer, follow them.

Always wash white and coloured garments separately. If no washing instructions, proceed as follows:

Machine-wash: Use the special synthetic setting on your washing machine (if no special setting, use warm water) and a biological detergent.

At the end of the rinsing cycle stop the washing machine; do not spin the garments. Take them out of the machine soaking wet, place them on hangers, put them back into shape and drip-dry.

The garments can also be tumble-dried but the result is not as good.

When tumble-drying, use the spinning cycle of the washing machine, then tumble-dry on low or medium heat.

When dried remove immediately, place on hangers and put back into shape. Leave to cool off.

Hand-wash: in lukewarm water and biological detergent.

Do not wring or rub. Squeeze the water through the fabric.

Rinse in lukewarm water. Squeeze out the excess water gently. Place the garments on hangers (or roll in a towel to absorb moisture and then place on hangers), put back into shape and leave to dry.

Synthetic fibre sweaters can be machine-washed (following label care instructions), but turn them inside out to avoid fuzzy balls collecting.

Taffeta
Made of silk or synthetic fibres. If made of silk, it should be dry-cleaned. Synthetic taffeta can be washed gently in warm water and a mild detergent. Do not rub or wring.

Hang up to drip-dry. Iron while still damp on the wrong side.

Towelling
Made of cotton fibres, it can be machine- or hand-washed following label instructions.

After washing shake the towelling out lightly before hanging it to dry. Ironing is not needed.

Terry towelling is used for nappies. Machine-wash on a hot setting and use a fabric-softener.

Velvet
Cotton and silk velvet should be dry-cleaned. If washable as indicated on the label, follow instructions for *Corduroy*.

Iron velvet face downward on a very, very thick bath towel and press over the wrong side.

To clean velvet gently rub it with a cloth dipped in powdered magnesia. Then brush with a soft brush.

To clean velvet brush it with a solution of water (1 teacup) and ammonia ($\frac{1}{2}$ teacup).

To keep a velvet collar clean, after wearing it, rub it with a synthetic foam brush or a piece of synthetic foam.

To restore the flattened pile of velvet, cover a hot iron with a wet cloth and hold the velvet firmly over it. Or hold the velvet, stretched tight, over boiling water, or iron velvet face down on a bath towel.

Methylated spirit or surgical spirit on a clothes-brush will remove fluff and hairs and give a new look to dusty, tired velvet.

Viscose
Man-made fibre. Follow label instructions. When in doubt follow instructions for *Acetate*.

Viyella
A mixture of wool and cotton. Wash by hand in warm water and mild synthetic detergent or on woollen programme of a machine. It does not shrink.

Iron while still damp, preferably on the wrong side.

Voile
Very thin cotton or synthetic fabric. Wash according to instructions for the type of fibre.

Do not wring. Roll in a towel to get rid of moisture. Iron while still damp.

Wool
Careful treatment must be given to wool. Wool can be damaged when washed in water that is too hot, by sudden changes in water temperature, by alkalis in soap, by household bleach or by rubbing or wringing.

Some wools are machine-washable. Look for washing and drying instructions on the label when buying woollens or wool by the metre (directions are written on the end of the roll of fabric).

Hand-wash woollens in lukewarm water using a special wool detergent or a soapless detergent. Squeeze the water through the fabric gently. Rinse well again using lukewarm water.

A little ammonia added to the soapy water when washing woollens will help to clean them thoroughly.

Two tablespoons of vinegar in the last rinse will keep your woollens soft. This applies to silk garments also.

Woollens will feel wonderfully soft if you add 2 teaspoons of cream hair-rinse to the final rinse. Squeeze out the water, roll in a towel to absorb moisture. Shake the garment a little to restore the pile. Dry flat, on a towel, away from sunlight or artificial heat.

Woollens can be ironed while still slightly damp using a dry cloth between the woollen and the hot iron. Do not press heavily on the iron or it will mark.

White wool getting yellowish can be bleached by soaking it in a solution of hydrogen peroxide and lukewarm water until it is white again (4 tablespoons of hydrogen peroxide to 2 pints/1 litre of lukewarm water). Strengthen the solution if the wool is very yellow and rinse.

When your woollen garments have been washed in water that is too hot and they become hard and 'felted', wash them in warm water to which glycerine has been added ($1\frac{1}{2}$ tablespoons to $1\frac{3}{4}$ pints about 1 litre). Then rinse very thoroughly in warm water.

Oily wool should be washed in soapflakes only to prevent the oil escaping from the fibres.

The best softener for wool blankets is 2 tablespoons of olive oil or glycerine added to the last warm rinse.

General hints

Some fabrics and colours can be damaged by certain solvents or spirits, so always test a small corner of the fabric first (leave for 20 minutes).

When removing stains from fabrics, start from the edge of the stain and work towards the centre. This will prevent the stain spreading.

A simple rule for unknown stains on fabric: first rub the stain with cold water. If the stain persists, rub on a mixture of lemon juice and salt. If this has no effect, rub on bicarbonate of soda. If this also fails, dab the area with methylated spirit.

Always rinse the fabric after removing a stain, or rub it with a piece of cottonwool dampened in cold water, to remove all traces of spirit or solvent.

Liquid detergents are best to remove stains. When used on washable fabrics just dampen the stain, then work the pure liquid detergent well into the stain. Next wash in the usual way.

When liquid detergent is used on non-washable fabrics dilute the detergent with an equal quantity of water and work it in using a very small amount. If too much is used, rinse by sponging the stain with cold water, or by using a syringe or a medicine dropper to force the water through.

Another way for rinsing the stain is to dab it with alcohol, as it dries faster (for material not damaged by alcohol, of course).

Many small stains on fabrics will disappear simply by rubbing them gently with the same fabric (hem, small end of the tie, etc.). Persevere.

Sponging method: When the directions say to 'sponge' the stain proceed in the following manner:

Fold a clean cloth. Place the stained material over it, wrong side up if possible, so that the stain can be melted away without having to go through the material. With a moistened white fleece of cottonwool or a white cloth gently wipe the solvent into the stain. Change the pad underneath frequently (as soon as some of the stain has been absorbed). *Do not* rub hard or the stain might spread and the surface of the fabric be damaged. Blot dry.

On fabrics likely to form a ring, sponge with a pad hardly moistened and start from the edges of the stain going to the centre. Blot dry, place the fabric on the palm of one hand and rub over the area with the other; this will prevent a ring forming. Repeat the whole process if needed.

Rings on fast-coloured fabrics can also be removed by holding the area over some boiling water.

Stains

Acids
On all fabrics: First wash or sponge at once with running cold water; then dip or sponge the stain in, or with, a solution of 1 tablespoon of ammonia to $\frac{1}{2}$ pint/$\frac{1}{4}$ litre of cold water.

One tablespoon of bicarbonate of soda diluted in $\frac{1}{2}$ pint/$\frac{1}{4}$ litre of water can be used instead of the ammonia−water solution.

On all carpets: Proceed as above.

Adhesive
On all fabrics, washable and non-washable: Place a piece of cottonwool or any absorbent cloth on the right side of the stain. Then dab the wrong side with a piece of cottonwool dampened with some non-oily nail-varnish remover.

On man-made fibres: Do not use non-oily nail-varnish remover. Use pure amyl acetate.

On carpets: If the carpet is wool, dab the stain with non-oily nail-varnish remover. If the carpet is synthetic, or if in doubt, dab the stain with amyl acetate.

Copydex (latex adhesive)
On any fabric: If the stain is still not dried, wipe it off with a damp sponge or cloth. If dry, scrape off the surface carefully with some liquid stain-remover.

On carpet: Proceed as above.

Epoxy resin (i.e., Araldite)
On fabrics: Only fresh stains can be removed. Place a piece of cottonwool or an absorbent cloth on the right side of the stain, then dab the wrong side with some cottonwool dampened with cellulose thinners or methylated spirit.

51

On man-made fibres: Dab the stain as above using lighter fuel instead.

On carpet: If the carpet is wool, dab the stain with non-oily nail-varnish remover. If the carpet is synthetic, or if in doubt, dab the stain with amyl acetate.

Model-making cement
On fabrics: With a knife, carefully scrape as much cement as possible, so as not to spread the adhesive. Then dab the stain with a piece of cottonwool dampened with acetone or some liquid stain-remover (i.e., Beaucaire).

On man-made fibres: Use some pure amyl acetate to remove the stain.

On carpet: Proceed as for fabric. On synthetic, or if in doubt, dab with amyl acetate.

Alcohol
See under individual headings for wine and beer.

Alcoholic beverages
On fabrics: Blot spilled drinks straight away and sponge the fabric with cold water. If the stain persists, work a little liquid detergent into it, then rinse. Next sponge with some methylated or surgical spirit to remove any traces of detergent.

Another way is to rub the stain straight away with a sponge dampened in methylated or surgical spirit.

On man-made fibres: Rub the stain with a solution of methylated or surgical spirit (1 tablespoon) and cold water (2 tablespoons). If the stain persists, rub with an equal mixture of hydrogen peroxide and cold water.

On carpets: On a fresh stain, flush some soda from a syphon and blot well. Or sponge with cold water, blot well and shampoo if needed. On a dried stain follow the fabric instructions above.

On synthetic carpet: Follow the instructions for man-made fibres.

On wood: When the stain is dealt with immediately, first wipe up the spilled drink, then rub the stain with a soft cloth slightly dampened with ammonia or methylated spirit. For an old stain rub it with a paste made of cigar or cigarette ash and salad oil (or, better still, linseed oil). Rub over gently until it disappears. Then wax and polish with a soft cloth. If any faint white marks are left, rub it with the raw edge of a cut Brazil nut or a walnut.

Metal polish rubbed over the stain will also remove it. Work in the direction of the grain.

Sweet sticky marks on varnished wood will disappear if rubbed gently with some used coffee grounds, slightly warm. Wipe and polish.

Alkali
On all fabrics: First wash or sponge at once with running cold

water. Then dip or sponge with some white vinegar or lemon juice. Lastly rinse or sponge with cold water.

On carpets: Proceed as above.

Animal stains (excreta, urine, vomit)
On all washable fabrics: Scrape any surface deposit. Sponge with cold water, then soak in a biological detergent or a solution of borax (1 tablespoon) and warm water (1 pint/$1\frac{1}{2}$ litres) for more delicate fabrics. Leave to soak for an hour before washing.

On non-washable fabrics: Scrape any surface deposit. Blot dry with absorbent paper. Sponge with a solution of powdered borax (1 tablespoon) and warm water (1 pint/$\frac{1}{2}$ litre). Then sponge with clear water. Blot dry. Clean any remaining trace with some methylated spirit on a damp cloth.

On all carpets: Scrape any surface deposit. Blot dry with absorbent paper. Rub with a mixture of warm soapy water (1 pint/$\frac{1}{2}$ litre) and vinegar (2 tablespoons). Blot dry, then flush some soda water from a syphon. Blot dry again, and rub with a cloth dampened with ammonia. Leave to dry.

Another way to remove a urine stain is to blot dry and pour methylated spirit on to it. Rub well. Then pour a little more methylated spirit and dab gently. Raise the pile and leave to dry.

Antiperspirants, deodorants
On all fabrics: For light stains rub with an equal solution of vinegar and water.

Or wash or sponge the stains with warm water to which a little liquid detergent has been added. Rinse well with cold water.

For more persistent stains rub with methylated spirit or liquid stain-remover. Next, sponge first with ammonia, then with cold water.

Or rub it with some hydrogen peroxide. Then rinse.

On carpet: Proceed as above.

Ballpoint
See under *Ink*.

Beer
On washable fabrics and table linen: For fresh stains rinse through under cold water before washing as usual.

For dried stains on table linen or white cotton, soak for a few minutes in a weak solution of warm water and bleach. Then put straight into cold water to which a few drops of ammonia have been added. Next rinse well.

Non-washable fabrics and coloured fabrics: Sponge with a solution of hydrogen peroxide (20 vol.) (1 tablespoon) and warm water (5 tablespoons), or with a solution of vinegar

(1 tablespoon) and warm water (2 tablespoons). Then sponge with clear water or launder.

On man-made fibres: Sponge with a solution of borax (1 tablespoon) and warm water (1 teacup). Launder, or sponge with clear water.

On all carpets: Treat fresh stains with a spray from the soda syphon. Then blot well. But fresh stains should respond very well to simple clear warm water if there is no syphon. Treat old stains by rubbing them with methylated spirit or a solution of hydrogen peroxide (20 vol.) (1 tablespoon) and water (4 tablespoons). Next sponge with warm water to which a few drops of ammonia have been added.

On wood: See Alcohol.

Beeswax
On all fabrics: Dab the stain with turpentine, soaking it well. Then rinse well and wash, or sponge well.

On man-made fibres: Dab the stain with a solution of methylated or surgical spirit (1 tablespoon) and cold water (2 tablespoons), rinse well and wash.

On carpets: For wool carpet proceed as for fabric. For synthetic carpet, or if in any doubt, proceed as for man-made fibres. Sponge well with clear water to finish.

Beetroot
On all washable fabrics: Follow the instructions for *Fruits, fruit juices,* but sprinkle some powdered borax over the stain before pouring the boiling water.

Another way to remove fresh beetroot stains is: first, rinse out under cold running water; then dab the stain with methylated spirit; next, wash in the usual way.

For coloured fabric: Soak in a solution of borax (2 tablespoons) and warm water (2 pints/1 litre) until the stain disappears. Then launder.

On non-washable fabrics: Follow the instructions for *Fruits, fruit juices* on non-washable fabric.

On all carpets: For fresh stains first blot up any liquid with a sponge or a paper towel. Then sponge the area with lukewarm water or spray it with the soda syphon, leave for a minute, then blot up the liquid.

For old stains work undiluted liquid detergent into it. Then rinse well; or dab the stain with an equal mixture of water and methylated spirit; or soak the stain with an equal mixture of water and hydrogen peroxide (20 vol.). Rinse well.

Berries
Blackberry, blackcurrant, etc. See under instructions for *Fruits, fruit juices*.

Bird droppings
On all washable fabrics: A good soaking in some biological detergent before washing should remove the stain. If the stain persists, dab with hydrogen peroxide (20 vol.) (1 tablespoon) diluted in water (4 tablespoons). White cotton can be soaked in a solution of bleach (2 tablespoons) and warm water (1 gallon/4 litres).

On non-washable fabrics: First wipe or brush any deposit, then sponge with a mixture of ammonia (1 tablespoon) and water (1 teacup). Next sponge with white vinegar and rinse.

On carpets: Follow the directions for non-washable fabrics.

On canvas garden furniture: Wipe or brush any deposit, then rub the stain over with household soap and sprinkle with washing soda. Leave for half an hour. Rinse well. Repeat if necessary.

Blood
On washable fabrics: Fresh bloodstains should always be cleaned with cold water, as hot water makes the mark

permanent. Soak in cool water for a while and then wash in warm soapy water. If the stain still persists, soak the material in a solution of warm water (1 gallon/4 litres) and bleach (2 tablespoons), or soak the stained area in a solution of water (7 tablespoons), ammonia ($\frac{1}{2}$ tablespoon) and hydrogen peroxide (20 vol.) (1 tablespoon). Rinse well.

On non-washable fabrics: Sponge with a mixture of cold water ($\frac{1}{2}$ pint/$\frac{1}{4}$ litre) and ammonia (1 teaspoon). Rinse and blot well.

For dried stains place a clean pad underneath the stain and sponge lightly with hydrogen peroxide or ammonia. Rinse well and blot.

Another way is to spray some starch on the stain and leave it on for a few hours. Then brush it off and wipe it with warm soapy water. Rinse well. If any brown mark is left, dab some hydrogen peroxide (20 vol.) over it until it disappears. Rinse well again.

On silk, satin or crêpe-de-chine: Make a thick paste of starch or talcum powder and water, or spray some starch over the stain. Leave it to dry completely. Brush the starch off with a soft brush. The stain will have disappeared and no harm will have been done to the fabric.

A paste made of a crushed aspirin tablet and water instead of starch or talcum powder will also work. Leave long enough for the paste to dry.

On all carpets: Sponge the fresh stain immediately with cold water or, better still, flush some soda water from a syphon over it. Blot well afterwards and shampoo if needed.

Cover dried stains with a paste made of starch or talcum powder and then brush or vacuum clean. Repeat if necessary.

On wood: Sand the stained area with some very fine steel wool (0000 grade). Then rub with a cloth or apply with a fine brush some hydrogen peroxide (20 vol.) until the stain disappears.

Bottled sauces
On washable fabrics: Rinse the stain immediately under cold running water. Work some liquid detergent into the stain. Then rinse. If any traces remain, soak in a biological washing powder solution for a while. Then launder in the usual way. *Do not* soak silk or wool in biological detergent; dab any remaining traces with diluted methylated or surgical spirit (1 part) and water (2 parts). Rinse well.

Dried stains can be softened first with an equal solution of glycerine and warm water. Leave for an hour before treating with one of the above methods.

On non-washable fabrics and man-made fibres: First, sponge the stain with cold water; then work some liquid detergent into the stain and rinse it well; next, wipe with methylated spirit or surgical spirit or ammonia on a damp sponge. Rinse. If any traces remain, dab the stain with an equal solution of hydrogen peroxide (20 vol.) and water. Rinse.

On all carpets: Scoop the excess and wipe with a damp cloth. Sponge with some warm water, then blot. Next sponge with a solution of water ($\frac{1}{2}$ pint/$\frac{1}{4}$ litre), liquid detergent (1 table-spoon) and white vinegar (2 tablespoons). Rinse and blot. Raise the damp pile. Leave to dry or dry with a hair-drier. If any traces remain, wipe with some methylated or surgical spirit. Rinse.

Brandy
Follow instructions for *Alcoholic beverages*.

Butter
Follow instructions for *Grease, oils, fats*.

Candle wax
On all fabrics: First remove as much as possible with the blade of a blunt knife, or if possible put the garment in the freezer for an hour. You can then break the frozen pieces off. Next place the stain between two sheets of blotting-paper and press with a warm iron, moving the paper frequently until no more grease appears on it. Sponge any remaining traces with some dry-cleaning fluid, some methylated or white spirit (but not on acetate fabric). Sponge with clear water.

For heavy fabrics another method is to stretch the stained fabric over a container and pour boiling water through the stain. Dry, and remove any remaining marks with some dry-cleaning fluid, methylated or white spirit.

On all carpets: Scoop the wax as much as you can with a spoon. Then place a sheet of blotting-paper or a few layers of tissue paper over the stain. Apply the pointed end of a warm iron only. Keep moving the paper frequently until no more grease appears on it. Remove any remaining traces with some

60

dry-cleaning fluid, methylated spirit or white spirit on a soft dry cloth. Sponge with clear water.

On polished wood: Hold a plastic bag with some ice cubes in it over the wax to harden it. Next, with a plastic spatula, your fingernail or a stiff card, scrape away as much of the wax as you can. Then wash off any remaining film with some warm soapy water to which a little vinegar has been added. Dry and polish. If any traces remain, gently rub with lighter fuel. Dry and polish.

On wallpaper: Do not scrape the wax for fear of tearing the wallpaper. Place a sheet of blotting-paper over the stain and press with a warm iron, moving the paper frequently. Remove any remaining traces by covering the stain with a paste made of french chalk or talcum powder and methylated spirit. Leave to dry. Brush off.

On vinyl wallcovering: Leave the wax to harden entirely before lifting it off with your fingernail, a plastic spatula or a thick card. Remove any remaining colour from the wax by dabbing lightly with methylated or surgical spirit.

Car oil
Follow instructions for *Grease, oils, fats*.

Car polish
On all fabrics: Remove with dry-cleaning fluid or methylated spirit. Next sponge with some liquid detergent, then rinse.

Caramel
On all fabrics: Sponge with cool water and a little detergent. Rinse. Let it dry. If any grease traces remain, sponge with a solution of ammonia or hydrogen peroxide (20 vol.) or methylated spirit and water in an equal quantity.

Carbon paper
On washable fabrics: Use undiluted liquid detergent and work it into the stain. Rinse well. If any traces remain, apply a few drops of ammonia or methylated spirit. Rinse well. Repeat if needed.

Non-washable fabrics and man-made fibres: Dab the stain with methylated or surgical spirit (1 part) and water (2 parts). If any traces remain, rub with a little liquid detergent and rinse. Repeat if needed.

On carpets: On wool carpet use the method for washable fabrics. On synthetic, or if in doubt, use the method for man-made fibres.

Carrot juice
Follow instructions for *Grass*.

Cat's puddle
See *Animal stains*.

Cherries
See *Fruits, fruit juices*.

Chewing gum
On all fabrics: Place the garment in the freezer for an hour; the chewing gum will then crack and can be picked off easily. Treat any remaining traces with methylated spirit or white spirit. If it

cannot be put in the freezer, hold a plastic bag with a few ice cubes in it over the chewing gum to harden it, then pick it off.

Another method is to saturate the stain with a liquid stain-remover. Repeat if needed. Sponge with cold water.

Yet another method is to hold the back of the stained fabric over the steam from a kettle. The gum will become soft and can be pulled off easily by hand or with tweezers.

On all carpets: Use one of the above methods.

On hair: Rub a plastic bag with some ice cubes in it over the gum until it becomes hard and can be picked off easily.

Another effective method is to rub the gum with some paint-brush cleaning solvent or peanut butter.

On vinyl upholstery: Scrape as much as possible. Then rub with some lighter fuel or kerosene.

Chocolate
On washable fabrics: Soak and wash in a biological detergent. If any of the stain remains, stretch the stained fabric over a container, sprinkle the stain with powdered borax and pour boiling water through the stain. Rinse, or dab any remaining stain with a liquid stain-remover.

On non-washable fabrics and man-made fibres: Sponge with lukewarm water, then with a solution of powdered borax (1 teaspoon) and warm water (1 teacup). Rinse and blot dry. Clear any remaining traces with a pad of cottonwool which has been first dampened with water then squeezed and dipped in methylated spirit or surgical spirit or ammonia.

On non-washable fabrics: Old stains should be loosened first by dabbing an equal solution of glycerine and warm water over the stain. Leave it for at least an hour. Rub with a sponge wrung out in warm water. Blot dry.

On all carpets: Blot up as much as possible. Flush some soda from a syphon over the stain. Blot up; when dry remove any remaining traces with some liquid stain-remover or some methylated or surgical spirit. Shampoo if needed.

Or blot the stain with absorbent paper first. Then dab with an equal mixture of white vinegar and methylated spirit. Sponge with clear water. Blot dry.

Chutney
On all washable fabrics: Sponge the stain with clear water. Then launder.

Old stains will need to be soaked in a borax (1 tablespoon) and warm water (1 pint/ $\frac{1}{2}$ litre) solution for an hour before laundering, or soaked in some biological detergent for an hour before laundering. This treatment is for stronger fabrics.

On non-washable fabrics: Scrape any surface deposit. Sponge the stain with clear water. Then rub with a pad of cottonwool which has been first dampened in water, then squeezed and dipped in methylated spirit or ammonia.

On all carpets: Scrape off any surface deposit. Sponge with warm water. Wash with carpet shampoo or a liquid detergent. Blot off. Then dab with some methylated spirit if any coloured stain remains.

Coca-Cola
On all fabrics: Sponge with cold water. Rub with a little liquid detergent. Rinse well. If any traces remain, treat with a solution of methylated spirit (2 tablespoons) and white vinegar (1 teaspoon). Rinse well.

Cocoa
Follow instructions for *Chocolate*.

Cod liver oil
On all washable fabrics: Treat the stain immediately before it

dries. Sponge the stain with some liquid stain-remover or methylated or surgical spirit. Then wash in the usual way.

Dried stains are difficult to remove. First remove as much as you can with some liquid stain-remover. Then loosen any remaining traces with a solution of an equal quantity of glycerine and warm water. Leave for at least an hour. Rinse and wash in the usual way. Bleach stubborn marks by dabbing them with a solution of hydrogen peroxide (20 vol.) (1 tablespoon) and cold water (4 tablespoons). Rinse.

On non-washable fabrics: Sponge the stain with liquid stain-remover.

On woollen garments: Put liquid detergent on the fresh stain. Rub lightly between the hands. Rinse well and wash as usual.

On all carpets: Blot the excess and sponge with a liquid stain-remover. Then wash with a dry-foam carpet shampoo. If a lot of cod liver oil has been spilled, it may be necessary to repeat this treatment after a few days.

Coffee
Follow instructions for *Chocolate*.

Stain inside coffee-pots or tea-pots/porcelain, earthenware
Rub it with salt or bicarbonate of soda.

For a badly stained tea-pot put one heaped teaspoon of washing soda into the pot and fill it up with warm water. Leave to soak for at least twelve hours before emptying and rinsing.

Another efficient way is to place some effervescent tablets used for cleaning dentures into the stained pot. Fill it up with boiling water and leave to cool. Rinse well.

A bleach solution ($\frac{1}{2}$ teacup of bleach to 1 pint/$\frac{1}{2}$ litre of water) will also clean the inside of a china or earthenware tea-pot.

On chromium
To take the tannin out of your chromium tea- or coffee-pot, rub it with a cloth dampened with vinegar and dipped in salt. Rinse well, as salt left on chromium will damage it after a while.

On glass
To clean a glass coffee-pot, first wet the inside of the pot, sprinkle it with salt, then place 10−20 ice cubes in the pot and swirl them around for a few minutes. Rinse and dry.

On marble
For slight drink stains (coffee, tea, fruit juice) on a marble table-top, use pumice powder or powdered chalk, rubbing it firmly over with a strong cloth. Rinse and dry.

On plastic
Coffee or tea stains on plastic will disappear if rubbed with nail-polish remover.

Correction fluid (Tippex)
On fabrics: Dab the stain with acetone or nail-varnish remover.

On man-made fibres: Dab the stain with amyl acetate.

On carpets: Follow the above instructions.

On synthetic carpet/or if in doubt: Follow instructions for man-made fibres.

Cosmetics (all types)
On washable fabrics: Work liquid detergent into the stain. Rinse well. Repeat if needed. Wash in the usual way — or blot the stain, then soak for a few minutes in a solution of ammonia (1 tablespoon) and warm water (1 pint/ $\frac{1}{2}$ litre). Rinse and wash.

Treat dried stain before washing by dabbing it with an equal solution of glycerine and warm water. Leave for an hour. Wash in the usual way.

On non-washable fabrics: Blot up any excess. Sponge with liquid stain-remover — eucalyptus oil, ether or methylated spirit. For man-made fibres dilute the methylated spirit with equal proportion of water. If any traces remain, work some powdered detergent into it. Rinse and blot dry.

On silk: Blot up any excess. Rub some french chalk or talcum powder into the stain. Leave for 2–3 hours. Brush off. If any traces remain, spray with an aerosol stain-remover.

On all carpets: Follow the instructions for non-washable fabrics.

On wood: Lipstick on light wood: rub the stain with toothpaste.

Cough mixture
Follow instructions for *Medicine*.

Crayon
On fabrics: Follow the directions for *Cosmetics*.

On wallpaper: First make a test on a hidden corner. Sponge gently with some liquid stain-remover. Leave to dry. Repeat if

needed. If a ring appears after the cleaning fluid has dried, cover it with a paste made of french chalk or talcum powder with some liquid stain-remover. Leave to dry. Brush off.

Another way is to rub the stain with some bicarbonate of soda on a damp cloth.

On vinyl wallpaper: Rub the stain with some silver polish.

On lino and vinyl floors: Rub with silver polish.

Cream sauce (edible)
On all washable fabrics: Follow instructions for *Grease, oils, fats.*

On non-washable fabrics: Scrape the excess. Sponge with warm water. Leave to dry, then sponge with a liquid stain-remover.

On all carpets: Follow the treatment for non-washable fabrics. Then wash with a dry-foam carpet shampoo.

Cream soup
Follow directions for *Cream sauce.*

Creosote
On all washable fabrics: First dab the stain with eucalyptus oil or liquid lighter fuel. Then wash as usual.

Dried stains should be loosened up before washing by rubbing in an equal solution of glycerine and warm water. Leave on for at least an hour before washing.

On non-washable fabrics: It is advisable to send the garment to a professional cleaner.

Curry
On all washable fabrics: On white material the fresh stains should be soaked for at least an hour in an equal solution of methylated spirit and water or ammonia and water, before being laundered in a biological detergent.

Another method is to rinse the stain in lukewarm water, then rub an equal solution of glycerine and water into the stain. Leave for at least an hour. Rinse, then soak the garment for another hour in some biological detergent before washing. If any traces remain, dab the stain with some diluted hydrogen peroxide (20 vol.) (1 tablespoon) and water (4 tablespoons).

On non-washable fabrics: Dab the stains with some ammonia or methylated spirit on a piece of cottonwool. Test coloured material first to make sure the alcohol does not affect the colour.

On man-made fibres: Dab the stain with an equal solution of methylated spirit or ammonia and water. Rinse.

On carpets: Blot up, then rub the stain with some methylated spirit or ammonia. Test the colour first in an inconspicuous place.

Another method is to blot up, then dab the stain with a solution of borax (1 tablespoon) and warm water (1 pint/ $\frac{1}{2}$ litre). If any traces remain, work some glycerine into the stain. Leave for 15 minutes. Sponge wtih warm water. Blot dry. Restore the pile by combing it with a fine clean comb.

Cycle oil
Follow instructions for *Grease, oils, fats.*

Dandelion
Follow instructions for *Grass.*

Deodorants
Follow instructions for *Antiperspirants.*

Drinks
Follow instructions for *Alcoholic beverages* or individual entries.

Duplicating ink and powder
See under *Ink.*

Dyes
On washable fabrics: Rinse immediately under cold water. Then work undiluted liquid detergent into the stain, then rinse. Repeat if needed and dab with some ammonia. Rinse and sponge with some methylated spirit.

On silk and wool: Dab or soak with, or in, a solution of hydrogen peroxide (20 vol.) (1 tablespoon) and cold water (5 tablespoons). Rinse well and wash.

On non-washable fabrics: Sponge with a solution of methylated spirit (2 tablespoons) and ammonia (1 teaspoon).

On man-made fibres: Follow the instructions for washable

fabrics. If any traces remain after washing, dab with a solution of methylated spirit (1 tablespoon) and water (2 table-spoons).

Egg

On all washable fabrics: Scrape off any deposit. Then wipe the stain with cold salted water. Then wash in the usual way. Do not use hot water to wipe the stain as it would set it.

Soak a dry stain in a biological detergent before washing.

On non-washable fabrics: Scrape off any deposit. Sponge the stain with some cold salted water. Rinse with clear, cold water. Leave to dry, or dry with hair-drier. If any traces remain, sponge with some liquid stain-remover.

On all carpets: Scrape any deposit. Sponge with some liquid stain-remover. Then shampoo if needed.

Egg stains on cutlery
Egg stains on cutlery can be removed by soaking the spoon or
fork in the water the egg has been boiled in. Egg tarnish on
silver is quickly removed by rubbing with table salt, wet earth or
a cooked potato.

Embroidery transfer
On all fabrics: Dab gently with methylated spirit before
washing.

On man-made fibres: Dab gently with an equal solution of
methylated spirit and water, then wash.

Engine oil
Follow instructions for *Grease, oils, fats.*

Epoxy resin
See under *Adhesives.*

Eye make-up
Follow instructions for *Cosmetics.*

Eyebrow pencil
On all fabrics: Rub with some liquid stain-remover on a
cottonwool bud or some cottonwool wrapped around an
orange-stick. Then dab with ammonia. Next sponge with
water.

Fat
Follow instructions for *Grease, oils, fats.*

Felt-tip pen
See under *Ink.*

Fish oil
Follow instructions for *Cod liver oil.*

Flower stains
Follow instructions for *Grass.*

Fly paper
On washable fabrics: Launder.

On non-washable fabrics: Wipe with liquid stain-remover.

Fly stains
On all fabrics: Sponge with some methylated spirit or some liquid stain-remover.

On man-made fibres: Sponge with an equal solution of methylated spirit and cold water. Or dab with some liquid stain-remover.

On light-shades: Rub inside and outside with a sponge squeezed in some warm biological detergent solution. Sponge with clear water. Blot well and leave to dry away from heat.

Foliage
Follow instructions for *Grass.*

Food colouring
On all fabrics: Sponge fresh stains immediately with cool water. Then work some undiluted liquid detergent into the stain and rinse. Next sponge with some methylated spirit.

On man-made fibres: Dilute the methylated spirit (1 part) with water (2 parts). If any traces remain, dab with some hydrogen peroxide (20 vol.). Then rinse.

On all carpets: Follow the above instructions.

Foundation cream
Follow instructions for *Cosmetics.*

Fountain-pen ink
See under *Ink.*

French polish (shellac)
On all fabrics: Dab with methylated spirit.

73

On man-made fibres: Dilute the methylated spirit in equal quantities of water.

On all carpets: Follow the above instructions.

Fruits, fruit juices
On all washable fabrics: Do not use soap and water or it will set the stain. Rinse with cold water, then stretch the stained fabric over a container and pour boiling water through the stain. If any traces remain, rub with some ammonia followed by diluted hydrogen peroxide (20 vol.) (1 part hydrogen peroxide, 5 parts water), or work an equal solution of glycerine and warm water into the stain. Leave for at least an hour and wash in the usual way.

If the above method of stretching the fabric over a container is not possible, then rinse with cold water, work some liquid detergent into the stain, leave the garment to soak for a few hours and then wash.

If the stain is old, cover it with powdered borax before pouring boiling water over it; or soften the stain first with an equal solution of glycerine and warm water. Leave for at least an hour. Then treat with boiling water.

On non-washable fabrics: Sponge with cold water, work some liquid detergent into the stain and rinse. If any traces remain, dab with ammonia and then with some diluted hydrogen peroxide (20 vol.) (1 part hydrogen peroxide, 5 parts water). Rinse and blot dry.

Another method is to dab the stain with white vinegar, and sponge with cold water.

Another method is to dab the stain with cold water and then cover with bicarbonate of soda. Leave on for 15 minutes. Brush off and leave to dry.

On all carpets: Blot up with a paper towel, then shampoo. If any traces remain, dab with methylated spirit.

On your hands: To remove stains from your hands after peeling a large quantity of apples, just rub the stains with apple peel and then wash your hands.

On marble: See under *Coffee*.

Furniture polish
Follow instructions for *Grease, oils, fats.*

Gin
Follow instructions for *Alcoholic beverages.*

Glue (animal and fish glues; for any other glue, see under Adhesives)
On all fabrics: Soak or dab the stain with warm white vinegar. Rinse and wash in the usual way, or rinse and blot dry or dry with a hair-drier.

Another method is to sponge with cold water, treat with ammonia. Rinse and blot dry or dry with a hair-drier.

On all carpets: Follow the above methods, or dab the stain with some non-oily nail-varnish remover.

Grape
Follow instructions for *Fruits, fruit juices.*

Grass
On all washable fabrics: Dab some methylated spirit on the stain, then rinse and wash in the usual way.

Another way is to work some liquid detergent into the stain. Then rinse. If any traces remain, treat with some hydrogen peroxide (20 vol.), then rinse.

On non-washable fibres: Sponge with diluted methylated spirit (1 part methylated spirit, 2 parts water). Test colours first on an inconspicuous area of the garment.

On all carpets: Foliage or flower stains will be removed if dabbed with methylated spirit.

Gravy
On all washable fabrics: Soak in cold water for half an hour, then wash in the usual way. If any traces remain, treat with a liquid stain-remover or a dry stain-remover.

Dried stains on table linen should be soaked in a biological detergent solution (follow instructions on the packet). Then wash.

On non-washable fabrics: Sponge with cold water, then sponge with some liquid stain-remover.

On all carpets: Scoop and blot up any excess. Treat with some liquid stain-remover. Then shampoo.

Grease, oils, fats
Eucalyptus oil will remove grease spots on any fabric, even the most delicate, without leaving any traces. Sponge lightly with water.

On all washable fabrics: First treat with some dry-cleaning fluid or methylated spirit. Then wash in warm soapy water.

Or rub the stain with some dry household soap or some pure liquid detergent before washing. If any traces remain after laundering, rub with some dry-cleaning fluid, or methylated spirit, surgical spirit or ammonia.

On non-washable fabrics: If the stain is fresh, spread a layer of talcum powder over it and gently press with your fingers. When the talcum becomes caked, brush it off. Then spread another layer and leave it overnight. Or spray with a dry-clean stain-remover before leaving overnight.

A quicker way is to place blotting-paper underneath the stain, sprinkle the stain with talcum powder, cover it with another sheet of blotting-paper, then press with a hot iron. Do not use this method for velvet.

On velvet: Drop a little turpentine over the stain, then rub with a soft cloth until dry. Repeat if necessary, then brush the pile well and air it for a while.

On silk: A small, fresh stain can be removed if gently rubbed with a piece of the same fabric (hem of dress or blouse, the narrow end of a tie). Persevere as this takes time. The soft part of a piece of bread rubbed over the stain is also good, or rub a lump of magnesia (powdered magnesia and water) over the stain. Leave to dry and then brush off. For older stains use the method for non-washable fabrics above.

On all carpets: Follow the instructions for non-washable fabrics. Shampooing may be necessary afterwards.

On leather: Rub the stain with dry-cleaning fluid, or cover the stain with some rubber adhesive, i.e., bicycle-puncture repair adhesive. Leave for at least 24 hours, then roll it off under your fingers. On light-coloured leather, test the rubber adhesive over a small surface area first, as it may stain. Polish and buff. Another way is to make a paste with some powdered chalk and methylated spirit. Apply to the stain, leave to dry and then brush off.

Grease or oil on suede shoes can be difficult to remove. Cover the stain with a paste made of cleaning fluid and salt and leave for a few hours. Repeat if the stain is stubborn.

On vinyl upholstery: Remove immediately with lighter fuel or turpentine to prevent a permanent stain.

On suede: Rub the stain lightly with liquid lighter fuel.

On wallpaper: Spray or paste the stain with starch or corn starch. Leave to dry and brush off. Repeat if needed.

Or place some blotting-paper over the stain and press with a warm iron.

If any marks remain, apply a paste made of talcum powder and methylated spirit. Leave to dry, then brush off.

Another way is to make a thick paste with talcum powder and a little liquid soap. Cover the stain and leave to dry. Then brush off.

On tile floors: To remove very dirty dark grease marks on floors, first scrape as much as possible with a knife, then rub some fat (butter, lard, salad oil) into the stain to soften it. Rub with methylated spirit or paraffin or white spirit. Lastly wash with warm soapy water.

On wooden floors: Dab the stain with methylated spirit. Next coat with talcum powder, cover with some blotting-paper and press with a warm iron. If the stain is old, repeating the operation might be necessary.

On wood: Sprinkle salt as soon as the stain appears to prevent the grease sinking into the wood.

Thickly coat the stain with some talcum powder or fuller's earth. Cover it with some blotting-paper or many layers of tissue paper, then press with a warm iron. Move the paper in such a way that there is always some clean part over the stain and use large enough paper not to touch the wood with the iron. Repeat until the heat has drawn all the grease out of the wood, on to the paper.

Another method is to rub the stain first with turpentine for a few seconds. Next cover with talcum powder. Then take a hot iron and hold it over the stain as near as possible without touching it, for a few minutes. Wipe away the talcum powder. Repeat if needed. If not, wax and buff.

On polished wood: First rub the stain with some hot milk. Wait a few minutes, then rub with a soft cloth dampened with a little vegetable oil or, even better, linseed oil. Then wash and buff.

On oak: Rub the stain with beer.

On marble: The stain is dark grey in the centre, getting lighter around the edges. To remove it apply over the stain a thick paste made of whiting (Spanish white from hardware stores) or powdered chalk and benzine or acetone, methylated spirit, white spirit or lighter fuel. Cover with a plastic film to hold in the moisture, then leave until it starts getting dry. Rinse and repeat if needed. If no whiting or powdered chalk is available, use a piece of blotting-paper.

On stone: Oil stains can be removed with clean blotting-paper sheets soaked in hot distilled water, reduced to a pulp and left to dry. Soak in white spirit, place over the stain in a thick coat (1−1½ inches/25−40 mm) and leave to dry. The blotting-paper will draw the oil stain out of the stone while drying. Light oil stains will come off if covered with a thick paste made from water and fuller's earth, Leave to dry.

On paper: First dab the stain with ether, then place the stained paper immediately between two sheets of blotting-paper. Leave to dry.

On wicker: Grease stains on wicker will be removed if rubbed with methylated spirit.

Hair dye
On all washable fabrics: Treat immediately, as most hair dye will be difficult to remove when dried. First sponge, then work liquid detergent into the stain, next dab with white vinegar, then more liquid detergent before washing in the usual way.

On non-washable fabrics: Sponge off any excess, then dab with some methylated spirit followed by hydrogen peroxide diluted in equal part of water. Blot dry.

Hair lacquer
On all fabrics: Dab first with some amyl acetate, then with some methylated or surgical spirit.

On mirror: Rub with a soft cloth dampened with methylated spirit.

Hair oil
On wallpaper: Follow instructions for *Grease, oils, fats* on wallpaper.

On vinyl: First wash with warm, soapy water. If any traces remain, rub gently with white spirit.

On fabric-covered headboards: Rub gently with some liquid stain-remover.

On wooden board: Wipe with a cloth moistened with liquid stain-remover or white spirit. Then polish.

Hand cream
On all washable fabrics: Rub in some liquid detergent, then rinse or wash in the usual way.

On non-washable fabrics: Treat with a stain-remover.

Honey
On all washable fabrics: Sponge with cold water, rub in some liquid detergent, then rinse.

On non-washable fabrics: Sponge lightly with cold water, then sponge with some hydrogen peroxide (20 vol.). Then wipe with a cloth wrung out in cold water.

On all carpets: Wipe with cold water first, then shampoo.

Ice cream
On all washable fabrics: Scrape and wipe off excess, then soak in a warm biological detergent. If any grease traces remain, treat with a liquid stain-remover. For final traces use hydrogen peroxide (20 vol.). Rinse.

On silk and wool: Do not soak. Sponge the stain with a solution of borax (1 teaspoon) and warm water ($\frac{1}{2}$ pint/ $\frac{1}{4}$ litre). Next wash as usual. Treat any remaining grease traces with liquid stain-remover. For final traces use diluted hydrogen peroxide (20 vol.) (1 part) and water (2 parts).

On non-washable fabrics: Scrape and wipe the excess. Sponge with lukewarm water, leave to dry. Remove any remaining stain with a liquid stain-remover. For final traces use some diluted hydrogen peroxide (20 vol.) (1 part) and water (2 parts).

On all carpets: Scrape and wipe off any surface deposit, then shampoo. Treat any remaining stain with a liquid stain-remover.

Ink
Ballpoint ink
On fabrics: Dab with methylated spirit on a cottonwool bud. Rinse. Wash the fabric if possible. Seek professional treatment for delicate fabrics.

On polyester (dacron, diolene, linelle, terylene, trevira): Spray

some hair lacquer generously on the stain. Leave for a minute, then rub well with a clean cloth. Repeat if needed.

On all carpets: Dab with methylated spirit. Rinse and blot dry. On all synthetic carpets spray the stain generously with some hair lacquer. Leave to dry. Then brush lightly with a soft brush and a solution of water and white vinegar in equal quantities. Blot dry. Raise the nap.

On leather: Dab the stain with some methylated spirit or an 'EFFLAX' pen used by schoolchildren.

On suede: Rub the stain with some fine sandpaper or a type-writer ink-eraser.

On wallcovering and vinyl surfaces: Do not wait as the stain would become permanent. Brush the mark with a soft nail-brush or a toothbrush and some warm soapy water.

On oilcloth: Rub the stain with a solution of vinegar and methylated spirit in equal proportions.

Duplicating ink
On all fabrics: Dab with white spirit. Next rub in some liquid detergent or neat washing-up liquid. Rinse. Repeat if needed. Wash if possible.

Duplicating powder
On all washable fabrics: Brush with a soft brush or vacuum. If any stain remains, wash in lukewarm soapy water. Do not use hot water or any solvent.

On non-washable fabrics: Brush off with a soft brush or vacuum. If any stain remains, seek professional advice.

On all carpets: Follow the instructions for non washable fabrics above.

Felt-tip ink
On all fabrics: Dab the stain with methylated spirit on a cotton-wool bud. (Do not use on acetate fabric and triacetate.) Then rinse or wash if possible.

Another way is to work some glycerine into the stain before washing in the usual way. If any stain remains, sponge with some methylated spirit. For acetate and triacetate use an equal part of methylated spirit and water.

On all carpets: Follow the above instructions.

On wallcovering and vinyl surfaces: Rub with some neat washing-up liquid, then rinse. Or dab with methylated spirit or lighter fuel.

Fountain-pen ink
On all washable fabrics: Rub the stain off under cold water as much as you can. Next stretch the stained fabric over a bowl, cover the stain with a good layer of salt and pour the juice of a lemon over it. Leave for at least 2 hours. Then launder.

Another way is first to blot the stain. Next soak it in some luke-warm salted milk until the stain disappears. Then wash.

On linen: Cover the stain with some tomato juice or a ripe tomato until the stain disappears. Then wash in lukewarm mild detergent solution.

Another method is to spread freshly made mustard over the stain. Leave for half an hour. Rinse and wash.

On wool: Place a pad underneath the stain and rub the spot with turpentine.

On non-washable fabrics: Blot up the stain. Dab the stain with a solution of hydrogen peroxide (20 vol.) in equal propor-tion with water or ammonia (1 tablespoon) and water ($\frac{1}{2}$ pint/ $\frac{1}{4}$ litre).

Another way is to blot up the stain, then sprinkle with some talcum powder, removing the powder as soon as it is stained, and repeat until the powder remains clear. Next make a paste with the talcum powder and some methylated or white spirit. Cover the stain and leave to dry. Brush it off. Repeat as many times as necessary.

On silk and wool: Stretch the stained area over a small con-tainer and put a drop of turpentine on the stain. Repeat from time to time until the ink disappears.

On all carpets: On fresh stains use the talcum powder method as above. Or flush the stain with soda water from a syphon, then blot with absorbent paper. Next sponge with warm water and blot again. Dry-foam shampoo the stained area and blot dry. Repeat if needed. If any traces remain, sponge with liquid stain-remover or methylated or white spirit.

Another method is to blot the stain as much as possible and then rub plenty of warm milk into it. Blot again and then sponge with warm water, to which has been added a little ammonia. Blot dry. Repeat if needed and shampoo.

Old stains will respond if sprinkled with salt and rubbed with half a lemon. Or pour lemon juice over it and rub with a cloth. Shampoo.

Or rub the old stain with some methylated or surgical spirit. Shampoo.

On fingers: A little tomato sauce will remove it.

On marble: When ink is spilled on marble, cover the spill immediately with fine salt. When the ink has been absorbed, wipe it off and cover the area with *sour milk.* Keep putting sour milk on as it dries, to keep it moist. It may take one or two days before the stain disappears completely.

On paper: Place blotting-paper underneath the stain and pour a few drops of hydrogen peroxide over it. Move the blotting-paper a little to get a dry part under the stain, then dab the stain with a piece of damp cottonwool to rinse it. Next place the wet paper between two layers of blotting-paper to dry it.

On silver: To remove ink stains from silver, make a paste with some chloride of lime and water. Rub the paste over the stain with a soft cloth until the stain disappears. Wipe the silver with a damp cloth (or wash if possible), dry and polish in the usual way.

On wood: See under 'red ink'.

Indian ink
On all fabrics: Dab the stain with some liquid stain-remover followed by some methylated spirit (dilute the methylated spirit for man-made fibres: 1 part of methylated spirit to 2 parts water). Then work a little liquid detergent into the stain. Sponge and blot dry.

On all carpets: Follow the above directions.

Marking ink
On all fabrics: Treat at once or it is practically impossible to remove. Dab with a liquid stain-remover. Repeat several times.

On all carpets: Follow the above instructions.

Printing ink
On all fabrics: Dab with methylated spirit (dilute the methylated spirit for man-made fibres: 1 part methylated spirit, 2 parts water). Next work some liquid detergent or washing-up liquid into the stain, then rinse.

On all carpets: Follow the above directions.

Red ink
Red ink is more difficult to remove, but try rubbing the stain with a paste made of borax and water. Rub any remaining traces with methylated or surgical spirit. Shampoo.

On lino/rubber/vinyl floors: Cover the stain for a few minutes with a cloth dampened in methylated or white spirit. Then wipe with a soft cloth dampened with ammonia. Do not use ammonia on lino.

Another way is to cover the stain with a cloth dampened in hydrogen peroxide (20 vol.) and leave it on until the stain disappears.

On leather: Rub some lemon juice over the stain. It will take some of the colour away, so use shoe polish to bring the colour back.

On wood: Rub the stains with a cloth dampened in vinegar and methylated spirit in equal quantities.

Another method is to apply a solution of oxalic acid (1 tablespoon) and warm water (1 teacup) over the stain with a brush. Wipe with a damp cloth, blot dry and polish.

Old stains are very difficult to remove. Dab the stain with a piece of cottonwool or a cottonwool bud and some household bleach. Then blot up with some absorbent paper. Repeat as many times as necessary, blotting up each time.

Another method is to rub the stain with some powdered pumice or rottenstone mixed to a paste with some linseed oil. Rub in the direction of the grain. Then wipe with some linseed oil. Repeat if needed, then polish.

On marble: See under 'Fountain-pen ink'.

On silver: Rub the stain with some chloride of lime mixed with water to a thick paste. (See under 'Fountain-pen ink'.)

On wallpaper: Blot up the stain immediately and carefully, so as not to spread it, put some talcum powder or french chalk or fuller's earth on a clean cloth and dab the stain with it. Brush off the absorbent powder as soon as it absorbs the ink and apply some more. Next make a paste with hydrogen peroxide (20 vol.) and some talcum powder, french chalk or fuller's earth. Cover the remaining stain with it. Leave to dry before brushing it off. This might take some of the colour, too.

Typewriter ribbon
On all fabrics: Dab with methylated spirit (dilute the meths with its equal quantity of water for man-made fibres) or a liquid stain-remover. Next work some liquid detergent, to which a drop or two of ammonia has been added, into the stain. Rinse. If any traces remain, sponge with some hydrogen peroxide (20 vol.), then rinse.

On all carpets: Follow the above instructions.

Iodine
On washable fabrics: Treat the stain immediately. Moisten the stain with water and place over the radiator, the steam from a boiling kettle or in the sun. Or soak in soapy water (4 pints/2

litres) to which 2 tablespoons of ammonia have been added. Then wash in the usual way. Or rub the fresh stain with a freshly cut lemon. Then wash.

On non-washable fabrics: Dab with methylated spirit. Then rinse with methylated spirit. Then rinse.

Or place a piece of cottonwool dampened in methylated or white spirit over the stain and leave for several hours. Moisten the pad with the alcohol from time to time.

On man-made fibres: Dab the stain with some methylated or white spirit diluted in water (1 part meths and 2 parts water).

On carpets: On wool use the method for non-washable fabrics above, then shampoo. For synthetics follow the instructions for man-made fibres. Then shampoo.

Jam
On all washable fabrics: Fresh stains will wash out. Soak old stains in a borax solution (1 teaspoon borax to 1 pint/ $\frac{1}{2}$ litre of warm water. Or work some liquid detergent into the old stain before laundering in the usual way.

On non-washable fabrics: Scrape off any excess, then sponge with some liquid detergent diluted in warm water. Rinse. If any traces remain, sponge with some hydrogen peroxide (20 vol.) diluted in its equal quantity of water and rinse.

Or rub a little powdered borax over the remaining stain. Leave for a few minutes, then rinse. Blot dry.

On all carpets: Scrape any excess. Wipe with a damp cloth. Then shampoo. If any traces remain, dab with methylated spirit. For synthetic carpets dilute the meths (1 part meths, 2 parts water).

Ketchup
Follow instructions for *Bottled sauces.*

Lacquer (nail varnish, transparent lacquers)
On all washable and non-washable fabrics: Blot up immediately with absorbent paper, place a pad underneath the stain, then dab the stain with acetone, amyl acetate or non-oily nail-varnish remover. If any traces remain, dab with some methylated spirit or some liquid stain-remover.

On man-made fibres: Dab the stain with amyl acetate. Nail-varnish remover might be used, if it does not contain acetone, so test first in an inconspicuous place.

On carpets: On wool use the treatment for washable and non-washable fabrics; then shampoo. For synthetics use the treatment for man-made fibres; then shampoo.

Lead pencil
On all fabrics: Rub with an eraser or dab with a liquid spot-remover. If any traces remain, soften with a solution of glycerine and warm water in an equal quantity. Sponge with some liquid stain-remover. Blot dry.

On all carpets: Follow the above instructions.

Leather marks
Leather rubbing against fabric can make marks very difficult to remove because of the tannin in the leather dye.

On all fabrics: Work some liquid detergent into the stain. Sponge and blot dry. Repeat if needed. If any traces remain, dab with some hydrogen peroxide (20 vol.).

Linseed oil
On all fabrics: Blot up any excess, then dab the stain with liquid stain-remover. Then work some liquid detergent into the stain. Sponge and blot dry or wash the article if possible.

Lipstick
Follow instructions for *Cosmetics*.

Liquors
Follow instructions for *Alcoholic beverages*.

Machine oil
On all fabrics and carpets: Rub with eucalyptus oil.

Mascara
Follow instructions for *Cosmetics*.

Mayonnaise
On all washable fabrics: Scrape off the excess and soak in a biological detergent, following the instructions on the packet. Launder.

On non-washable fabrics: Scrape off the excess and treat with a liquid stain-remover or an aerosol stain-remover.

On all carpets: Scrape off any excess and shampoo. If any traces remain, dab with liquid stain-remover or methylated spirit (dilute for synthetic carpets: 1 part meths to 2 parts water).

Meat juices
On all washable fabrics: Soak in biological detergent before washing.

On non-washable fabrics: Work some liquid detergent into the stain. Rinse and blot dry. If any traces remain, sponge with some liquid stain-remover.

Medicines
On all fabrics: If the medicine has a base of sugar syrup (i.e., cough medicine), wash out with soap and water if the fabric is washable. If it is non-washable, sponge it off and remove any remaining traces with methylated spirit, diluted with 2 parts water for man-made fibres.

If it is a *gummy* medicine, loosen the stain by rubbing some Vaseline, lard or butter into it, then sponge with a liquid stain-

91

remover. Rinse and blot dry, or launder if the fabric is washable.

On all carpets: Follow the above instructions.

Mercuro chrome
On all washable fabrics: Soak the fabric in a warm detergent solution to which some ammonia has been added (10 table-spoons ammonia to 4 pints/2 litres water) for at least 12 hours. If any traces remain, place a pad of cottonwool dampened in methylated spirit or white spirit over the stain. Keep the pad moist with the methylated or white spirit and leave it on until the stain disappears. Dilute the alcohol with 2 parts of water for man-made fibre.

On non-washable fabrics: Sponge the stains with methylated or white spirit. Dilute the alcohol (1 part alcohol to 2 parts water) for use on man-made fibres.

On coloured fabrics: Where alcohol cannot be used, rub some liquid detergent on the stain, next dampen a pad of cotton-wool with ammonia and dab it over the stain. Rinse with cold water. Repeat if needed.

On all carpets: Follow the above instructions.

Metal polish
On all fabrics: Wipe any excess. Next sponge off with water, work some liquid detergent into the stain, sponge with water again. If any traces remain, sponge with methylated spirit (diluted in 2 parts of water for man-made fibres). Rinse and blot dry.

On all carpets: Wipe any excess. Dab with methylated or white spirit. Leave to dry. Brush the powdery deposits. Shampoo if needed.

Metal stains
Stains caused by tarnished silver, copper, brass, etc., rubbing against fabrics.

On all fabrics: Wet the stain with lemon juice or white vinegar. Sponge with water. Blot dry. Bad stains can be removed by treating them with oxalic acid.

Mildew
On all washable fabrics: Fresh stains can be removed by laundering and if possible drying in the sun. If not, treat any remaining traces by dabbing them with a solution of hydrogen peroxide (20 vol.) (1 part) and cold water (3 parts). Diluted bleach (1 tablespoon of bleach to 1 teacup of water) can be used to dab the remaining traces on cottons or linens.

Another way is to soak the stain with buttermilk and leave in the sun to dry. Repeat until the mark disappears.

On coloured fabrics: Slightly wet the stain with cold water, then rub some household soap over it. Dry in the sun. Repeat until the mark disappears.

Small stains on any fabric can be removed by rubbing them with half a lemon dipped in salt. Then sponge with lukewarm water. Dry in the sun.

On non-washable fabrics: Seek professional advice.

Mildew on linen can be removed by rubbing the stains with a bar of soap when the linen is damp, then covering the soapy stains with powdered chalk. Rub the powder in well, wet it a little as it gets dry. Leave for 12 hours. Repeat the whole process if necessary.

On all carpets: Sponge with a carpet shampoo. Rinse with a clean damp cloth. Next rub the carpet with a mild bleach solution (1 tablespoon bleach to 1 pint/ $\frac{1}{2}$ litre of water). Dry with an electric fan.

On tiled walls, cement floors, tiled floors: Wash with a bleach solution (2 teacups of bleach to 4 pints/2 litres of water). Rinse with water and dry as much as possible.

On vinyl wallcoverings: Soak the stains with a solution of ammonia (1 teaspoon), hydrogen peroxide (20 vol.) ($\frac{1}{2}$ teacup) and water (1 teacup). Leave it on for 15 minutes. Rinse with water and blot dry.

On plastic shower curtains: Sponge the curtains with a bleach solution (2 tablespoons of bleach to 1 pint/$\frac{1}{2}$ litre of water). Rinse and dry.

Rub mildew stains on shower curtains with bicarbonate of soda.

On mattresses and upholstery: Take the article outside if possible and brush off the mould. Leave the article in the sun until thoroughly dry. If this treatment is not possible, sponge the stains with an equal solution of methylated or white spirit and water. Then dry thoroughly using an electric fan.

On leather: Rub the stains with petroleum jelly. Then polish.

Another way is to wipe the stains with some undiluted antiseptic mouthwash. Wipe dry, then wax and polish.

Yet another way is to rub the stains with an equal solution of methylated spirit and water. Dry well, then wax and polish. If the mildew is still remaining, wash it with some thick sud detergent. Rinse by wiping with a damp cloth and dry well. Wax and polish.

Or scrape the stain with very fine sandpaper, then rub with shoe polish the same colour as the leather.

On paper: Sprinkle the stain with talcum powder if it is damp. Leave it overnight, then brush off. Erase the stains by dabbing them with a small pad of cottonwool dampened with a solution of household bleach (1 teaspoon of bleach to 3 teaspoons of water), or with an ink eradicator. Blot dry.

95

In the kitchen, bathroom, etc.
To get rid of mildew spots in the kitchen, bathroom or laundry room rub the mildew with household bleach, using a toothbrush for stubborn parts. When the mildew is all gone, rinse thoroughly with clean water until no bleach is left, then wash with ammonia. This substance is dangerous, so always wear gloves. Painting over mildew will not get rid of it; it will eventually grow back. Kill the mildew before painting.

On stone
Mildew on porous stone (sandstone, limestone) can be removed with blotting-paper. First soak sheets of clean blotting-paper in hot distilled water, then reduce to a pulp and spread thickly (at least 1 inch/25 mm) over the mildew. As the paper dries it will draw the stain out with the water.

Milk
On all washable fabrics: Soak for a while in lukewarm water, then wash in the usual way. If any traces remain, sponge with a liquid stain-remover.

Non-washable fabrics: Sponge the stain with dry-cleaning fluid then sponge with lukewarm water.

Or soak the stain in methylated spirit in a saucer. Then sponge with lukewarm water. Do not use this method for man-made fibres.

On all carpets: Shampoo. If any traces remain, sponge with dry-cleaning fluid or methylated spirit.

Another way is to blot the milk as much as possible. Next flush the stain with soda water from a syphon, then sponge with lukewarm water. Blot dry. If any traces remain, rub in a little solution of carpet shampoo. Leave to dry.

Mud
On all washable fabrics: Wait until the mud is dry, then brush off as much as you can before laundering. If any traces remain, treat with a liquid stain-remover.

On coloured fabrics: If, after washing, the colour has faded, dip the stained part in a solution of ammonia (1 tablespoon) and water (6 tablespoons) for a little while. Rinse well.

On non-washable fabrics and upholstery: Wait until the mud is dry, then brush it off. Sponge the stain with a mild detergent solution. Wipe with a sponge squeezed out in cold water, and blot dry. If any traces remain, treat with a liquid stain-remover.

Another way is to wait until the mud is dry, then brush off. Next sponge the stain with a solution of methylated or surgical spirit and water in equal quantity. Or wipe the mark with water to which some bicarbonate of soda has been added (1 teacup water, 1 tablespoon bicarbonate of soda).

On raincoats: Wait until the mud has dried, then brush it off. Next sponge with water to which some vinegar has been added (1 teacup water, 3 tablespoons vinegar).

On all carpets: Wait until the mud is dry, then brush it off and

97

vacuum. If the stain remains, use a carpet shampoo. Leave to dry. Treat any remaining traces by dabbing them lightly with a cloth dipped in methylated spirit.

Mustard
On all washable fabrics: Laundering in a warm detergent solution should remove the stain. If any traces remain, sponge with an ammonia solution (3 tablespoons ammonia, $\frac{1}{2}$ pint/ $\frac{1}{4}$ litre water).

Dried stains should be loosened up before laundering by rubbing some glycerine solution (water and glycerine in equal quantities) into the stain. Leave for at least an hour, then launder.

On non-washable fabrics: Wipe with a cloth wrung out in water. Next sponge with a mild detergent solution and rinse. If any traces remain, wipe with an ammonia solution (3 tablespoons ammonia, $\frac{1}{2}$ pint/ $\frac{1}{4}$ litre water). Blot dry.

On all carpets: Scrape any excess, then shampoo. If any traces remain, dab with an ammonia solution (3 tablespoons ammonia, $\frac{1}{2}$ pint/ $\frac{1}{4}$ litre water).

On silver: Acid stains (i.e., mustard) are difficult to remove but will disappear if rubbed with salt and a few drops of lemon juice. Alternatively, soak the silver in hot vinegar for fifteen minutes.

Nail varnish
On all fabrics: Blot up the excess with absorbent paper. Then place a pad underneath the stain and dab with cottonwool dampened with non-oily nail-varnish remover or acetone. (Do not use non-oily nail-varnish remover on man-made fibres.) If any traces remain, sponge with methylated spirit.

On man-made fibres: Blot up excess with absorbent paper, then place a pad beneath the stain and dab with cottonwool dampened with amyl acetate.

On all carpets: Blot up excess with absorbent paper, then dab stain with cottonwool dampened with amyl acetate. Non-oily nail-varnish remover can be used on some carpets, but make a test first. If any traces remain, sponge with methylated spirit or white spirit. Finish the whole treatment by shampooing the area.

Nicotine
On all fabrics: Sponge the stain with some methylated or white spirit (dilute the alcohol with 2 parts water for man-made fibres).

Another way is to sponge with cold water and work a little liquid detergent into the stain. Rinse and blot dry. If any traces remain, dab with hydrogen peroxide (20 vol.) and water mixed in equal proportions.

On fingers: Rub fingers with a quarter of a lemon or with cottonwool dipped in hydrogen peroxide (20 vol.). Rinse your fingers immediately.

99

On china: Rub the stain with a slightly damp cork dipped in salt.

Oil
See *Car oil, Cycle oil, Grease, Hair oil, Paraffin oil*.

Ointment
On all fabrics: Dab with a liquid stain-remover. Rinse with cold water. If any traces remain, work some liquid detergent into the stain, then rinse and blot dry.

Orange juice
Follow instructions for *Fruits, fruit juices*.

Paint, varnish
Clean fresh stains immediately as it is very difficult to remove dried stains.

Oil paints, gloss, enamel paints, oil-based undercoat, varnish
On all washable fabrics. Dab with white spirit, a liquid stain-remover or commercial paint-brush cleaner. Rinse. Repeat if needed. Wash the garment if possible.

Another way is to rub the stain with a solution of turpentine and ammonia in equal quantity until the stain disappears. Next launder.

Treat dried stains with a special paint-remover. Test man-made fibres in an inconspicuous area first. Then wash.

On man-made washable fabrics: Dab with turpentine, then sponge with methylated or white spirit to remove the turpentine stain. Sponge with cold water and blot dry.

Dried stains should be loosened up by placing a pad dampened with turpentine for half an hour over it. Rinse. If any traces remain, work a little liquid detergent into the stain, then rinse. Repeat if needed by using the turpentine and liquid detergent alternately until the stain disappears. Dab with methylated or white spirit (dilute the alcohol for man-made fibres: 1 part alcohol, 2 parts water). Rinse and blot dry.

On all carpets: Dab with white spirit, liquid stain-remover or commercial paint-brush cleaner. Sponge with cold water. Repeat if needed, then shampoo.

Emulsion and water-based undercoat and paints
On all fabrics: Fresh stains can be washed off with cold water, then laundered if possible.

Dried stains need to be loosened up with methylated spirit (dilute the alcohol in equal parts with water to use on man-made fibres). Next wash in the usual way or sponge with warm water. If any traces remain, dab the wet stain with ammonia. Rinse well.

On all carpets: Follow the above instructions.

Cellulose paint
On all fabrics and carpets: Treat with acetone but not on man-made fibres. Instead use a liquid stain-remover or an appropriate thinner.

Acrylic paint
On all fabrics and carpets: Sponge with water then work some liquid detergent into the stain. Rinse. If any traces remain, dab with a liquid stain-remover or methylated spirit (do not use methylated spirit on man-made fibres).

Paraffin oil
Follow instructions for *Grease, oils, fats.*

Pencil, black and coloured
On all fabrics: Try to rub the mark with a pencil-eraser first. If it is not possible, rub with a liquid stain-remover. Sponge with a mixture of water and ammonia, half and half. Repeat the treatment if needed.

Perfume

On all washable fabrics: Gently rub the stain with white spirit. Then wash in warm soapy water.

Another way is to loosen the stain with a solution of glycerine and water in equal quantity. Leave for at least an hour, then wash.

On non-washable fabrics: Gently rub the stain with white spirit. Use diluted white spirit on man-made fibres (1 part white spirit, 2 parts water). If the stain persists, rub with hydrogen peroxide (20 vol.) and sponge with cold water immediately.

Another way is to loosen the stain with a solution of glycerine and water in equal quantity. Leave it on the stain for at least an hour. Wipe with a sponge squeezed in warm water. Blot dry.

On all carpets: Blot up as much as you can. Next dab with white spirit, then shampoo.

Perspiration

On all washable fabrics: Do not wash the garment until the stain has been treated. Soak the affected part in cold, very salty water for half an hour, then rub half a juicy lemon on it and let it soak in for a minute or two. Rinse and wash as usual.

If the colour has been changed by the perspiration, try to restore it by holding the fabric, first dampened with water, over the fumes of an open bottle of ammonia.

If it is a fresh stain, apply ammonia and white vinegar. For an old stain methylated spirit can also be used to restore colour, but do not use it on man-made fibres.

White cotton and linen can be bleached in a solution of methylated spirit and ammonia ($\frac{1}{2}$ teacup of methylated spirit, 1 teaspoon of ammonia). Soak until the stain disappears.

Or soak in a solution of hydrogen peroxide (20 vol.) and water (1 part hydrogen peroxide, 5 parts cold water).

On silk and wool: Dab or soak with a diluted solution of hydrogen peroxide (20 vol.) and water in equal quantities. Dab or soak for at least ten minutes before washing.

Non-washable fabrics: Sponge the stain with a solution of ammonia and water in equal quantities.

Pitch

Follow instructions for *Tar*.

Plasticine

On all fabrics and carpets: Scrape off any surface residue. Place an absorbent pad under the stain and dab the stain with some liquid stain-remover or lighter fuel (on man-made fibres test over an inconspicuous area first). Next wash washable fabrics or sponge non-washable fabrics with warm water and blot dry. Shampoo the carpet.

Plum
Follow instructions for *Fruits, fruit juices*.

Printing ink
See instructions for *Ink*.

Rain spots
On leather handbag: Hold the handbag over a container full of boiling water, not too close, for one or two minutes. Wipe well. Wait until well dry and then polish with natural-colour wax.

Another way is to rub the leather with a cloth dampened in cold soapy water. Rinse. Blot well, then polish.

On felt hat: Rub the spots with a crumpled tissue paper.

Raspberry
Follow instructions for *Fruits, fruit juices*.

Rosin
On all fabrics and carpets: Dab with one of the following products: liquid stain-remover, methylated or white spirit (dilute the alcohol with 2 parts water for man-made fibres), eucalyptus oil (for more delicate fabrics), liquid lighter fuel or ether. Dab the liquid on the wrong side to push the stain out, if possible. Rinse by sponging with cold water or launder. Old stains can be loosened up with a glycerine solution ($\frac{1}{2}$ warm water, $\frac{1}{2}$ glycerine) before washing.

On woollens: Place the stain over some talcum powder (the talc is then underneath the stain). Next dab with turpentine.

On fast-colour fabrics: Dab the stain with turpentine. Next sponge with methylated or white spirit (dilute in 2 parts water for man-made fibres).

Ribena
Follow instructions for *Fruits, fruit juices*.

Rum
Follow instructions for *Alcoholic beverages.*

Rust
On baths: Stains caused by a dripping tap should be rubbed with a paste made of salt and lemon juice and then rinsed. If the stains are old and resistant, make a paste of cream of tartar and peroxide. Rub the stain with a brush (an old toothbrush will do), rinse and hope for the best!

On iron or steel: A small stain on a delicate object can be removed with an ink-eraser. For more persistent stains on tougher objects, first soften the rust by dipping the object in paraffin for 24 hours. Then take it out of the paraffin, wipe it lightly and rub the metal with steel wool until clean. If it is not possible to dip the object, wrap the rusty part with a cloth soaked in paraffin and leave it for 24 hours. Then rub the metal with steel wool. Protect non-metal parts with plastic adhesive tape.

To remove rust marks from a steel draining board, rub with liquid lighter fuel.

On vinyl floor tiles: Wearing rubber gloves, rub in a weak solution of oxalic acid (1 tablespoon oxalic acid to 1 pint/ $\frac{1}{2}$ litre of warm water).

On linen: Place a little oxalic acid on a piece of white material. Knot the material into a small bag. Dip the bag in hot water and dab it on the stain. The mark will disappear immediately. Rinse in clean water.

Salad dressing
Follow instructions for *Grease, oils, fats.*

Sauce
See also under different headings for *Bottled sauces, Gravy, Mayonnaise, Mustard,* etc.

On all fabrics and carpets: When in doubt about the origins of the sauce, sponge with cold water. Work some liquid detergent or washing-up liquid into the stain. Sponge with cold water. Dab with methylated spirit (dilute the alcohol in 2 parts of water for man-made fibres). Sponge with cold water. Blot dry or wash.

Scent
Follow instructions for *Perfume*.

Scorch marks
When the fibres have been badly burnt scorch marks cannot be removed.

On all washable fabrics: Light scorch marks can be removed by sponging with hydrogen peroxide (20 vol.) or by rubbing the marks with a piece of sugar moistened with water. In both treatments sponge with cold water afterwards.

Another method for light scorch marks is to dampen the area with a glycerine solution (half warm water, half glycerine) and rub it fabric to fabric. Next soak in a solution of borax (2 tablespoons) and warm water (1 pint/$\frac{1}{2}$ litre). Leave until the scorch mark clears up. Rinse, then launder.

Another method is to place the stained fabric over a small container of boiling water. Make a paste with 2 teaspoons of fine salt and 2 tablespoons of lemon juice. Spread over the stain. Leave for a short while. Rinse with water. Repeat if necessary.

Another method is to cover the stain with a paste made of fine salt and lemon juice and leave it to dry in the sun, or hold it over the steam from a boiling kettle. Rinse well.

Yet another way is to boil the stained fabric or garment in a solution of water (4 pints/2 litres) and cream of tartar (4 tablespoons). Boil until the stain has disappeared. Rinse well.

On white cotton and linen: Stretch the stained fabric over a container and pour boiling water through the mark (from as high as possible without splashing). Next cover the stain with a paste made of white vinegar and cream of tartar or powdered borax. Leave for two minutes, then rinse in warm water to which a little ammonia has been added. Repeat if needed before laundering.

Very light fresh marks will respond well if dabbed with hydrogen peroxide (20 vol.) or lemon juice. Rinse immediately.

On non-washable fabrics: Follow the hydrogen peroxide (20 vol.) or sugar treatment above − or seek professional advice from a dry-cleaning specialist.

On all carpets: If the burn is small and light, rub it out with hydrogen peroxide (20 vol.) and leave to dry. Any burnt tips left can be trimmed with nail scissors.

For a small but deeper burn, cut as much as you can of the burnt part with small scissors, then cover it with a light coat of glue and patiently, with the help of tweezers, cover the glue with some pile of the same carpet cut from an inconspicuous corner. Leave to dry.

On wool: Light marks can be rubbed with very fine sandpaper or an emery board.

Sea-water marks
On all fabrics: Sponge with a solution of vinegar (1 part) and water (2 parts). Launder if possible.

On leather shoes: Dissolve a small piece of washing soda in four tablespoons of hot milk. While the mixture is warm apply it to the stain with a cloth, rubbing well. When dry, clean the shoe with your usual polish.

Another way is to rub white vinegar and warm water in equal proportions over the stain, then polish.

Sealing wax
On all fabrics and carpets: Dissolve the wax by dabbing it with methylated spirit or white spirit (dilute in 2 parts water for man-made fibres). Rinse and blot dry. Repeat if necessary.

Sewing machine oil
On all fabrics and carpets: Rub the spot with ammonia. Next wash or sponge with warm water and blot dry.

Shellac
Follow instructions for *Resin.*

Shoe polish
On all fabrics and carpets: Scrape off the surface residue, and dab with a liquid stain-remover. If any traces remain, dab with methylated or white spirit (diluted in 2 parts of water for man-made fibres). If after this treatment any stain remains, wipe with hydrogen peroxide (20 vol.). Sponge with cold water afterwards. Blot dry, or wash if possible.

Dried, difficult stains should be loosened first with a glycerine solution (half glycerine, half warm water). Work it well into the stain. Next dab with a liquid stain-remover. If any traces remain, sponge with methylated or white spirit (diluted in 2 parts of water for man-made fibres). Rinse and blot dry, or wash if possible.

On vinyl upholstery: Wipe away any excess, then rub with turpentine.

Soft drinks
Follow instructions for *Fruits, fruit juices*.

Soot
On all washable fabrics: Soak in cold water, then launder.

On non-washable fabrics: Shake or vacuum the stain. Do not brush to prevent spreading the soot. If any traces remain, dab with a liquid stain-remover or use an aerosol stain-remover.

On all carpets: Never wet a soot stain.

On light-coloured carpets: Cover the stain with salt, french chalk or fuller's earth, and vacuum. Repeat the process until the stain has disappeared.

On darker-coloured carpets: Vacuum the stain first and sponge away any remaining traces with a liquid stain-remover.

Spirits
Follow instructions for *Alcoholic beverages.*

Stove polish
On all washable fabrics: Work liquid detergent into the stain, then launder.

On non-washable fabrics: Apply salt or talcum powder over the stain. Work it into the fabric, then brush it off. Repeat until the stain has almost gone, then wipe with a liquid stain-remover.

Strawberry
Follow instructions for *Fruits, fruit juices.*

Suntan lotion
Follow instructions for *Grease, oils, fats.*

Syrup
Follow instructions for *Jam* or *Medicine.*

Tar
On all washable fabrics: Small stains on fabrics will be removed if dabbed with non-oily nail-varnish remover or acetone. Do not use those on man-made fibres. For larger stains work some butter, margarine, lard or glycerine into the stain with your fingertips. Leave on for a good hour. Next sponge with a liquid stain-remover, then launder.

Another way is carefully to scrape as much as possible, then dab with eucalyptus oil. Leave to dry before laundering.

On wool and silk: Scrape as much as you can, then treat with eucalyptus oil or ether. Next launder as usual.

On non-washable fabrics: Scrape as much as possible and treat with eucalyptus oil.

Another way is to loosen the stain with a glycerine solution (half glycerine, half warm water). Leave for an hour, sponge with cold water. Blot well and dab with a liquid stain-remover.

On all carpets: Scrape as much as possible. Loosen the stain with a glycerine solution (half glycerine, half warm water). Leave on for an hour. Rinse with water and blot well. When dry use a liquid stain-remover or an aerosol stain-remover on any remaining traces.

Another way is to scrape any excess, then cover the stain with a thick paste made of fuller's earth and turpentine. Rub it well into the stain. Leave to dry, then brush it off.

On feet and hands: Rub the stain with paraffin or with the outside of a lemon or an orange peel, or with oil or butter.

On leather: Dab the stain with liquid lighter fuel.

Tea
Follow instructions for *Chocolate*.

Tobacco
Follow instructions for *Nicotine*.

Tomato juice purée
Follow instructions for *Fruits, fruit juices*.

Treacle
Follow instructions for *Jam*.

Turmeric
This is a spice used in curry powder, mustard and pickles. Follow instructions for *Curry*.

Typewriter ribbon
See *Ink*.

Urine
On all washable fabrics. Rinse in cold water to which ammonia has been added (1 tablespoon ammonia to 2 pints/1 litre water), then launder in the usual way.

Soak dried stains in a biological detergent before laundering (follow instructions on the packet). Any yellow marks on cotton or linen can be bleached out by dabbing with a hydrogen peroxide (20 vol.) solution (1 part hydrogen peroxide to 5 parts cold water) to which a few drops of ammonia have been added.

On non-washable fabrics: Sponge with cold water. Blot dry. Then sponge with a vinegar solution (3 tablespoons vinegar to 1 pint/$\frac{1}{2}$ litre warm water). One might have to repeat the process for dried stains as they are difficult to remove.

On all carpets: Flush soda water from a syphon over the stain or sponge with an ammonia solution (2 tablespoons ammonia to 1 pint/$\frac{1}{2}$ litre warm water). If the colour has been changed and the ammonia solution does not help, sponge with white vinegar and blot dry.

112

On mattresses: Sponge with cold washing-up liquid solution. Wipe with cold water to which a dash of white vinegar has been added or a few drops of antiseptic (i.e., Dettol). Blot well and leave to dry in an airy place.

See also *Animal stains*.

Varnish
See instructions for *Paint*.

Vaseline
On all fabrics and carpets: Sponge with turpentine or a liquid stain-remover. Then wash or sponge with warm water.

Vegetable stains
Follow instructions for *Grass*.

Vinegar
Follow instructions for *Acids*.

Vodka
Follow instructions for *Alcoholic beverages*.

Vomit
On all washable fabrics: Scrape any surface deposit and rinse under cold running water. Soak in a biological detergent solution (following the instructions on the packet), then wash.

On non-washable fabrics: Scrape any surface deposit. Sponge with warm water to which a few drops of ammonia have been added. Blot dry.

Another way is to scrape off excess, sponge with warm water, then blot dry. Next sponge with a liquid stain-remover.

On all carpets: Scrape any excess, then flush some soda water from a syphon. Blot well. If no syphon water, sponge the stain with a borax solution (3 tablespoons borax to 1 pint/ $\frac{1}{2}$ litre warm water). Shampoo, rubbing well until the stain has gone.

113

Rinse with warm water to which a few drops of antiseptic have been added.

On mattresses: Remove any surface deposit. Sponge with a warm washing-up liquid solution. Sponge with cold water to which a few drops of ammonia have been added. Blot well and leave to dry in an airy place.

See also instructions for *Animal stains.*

Walnut
Dark brown stains are very difficult to remove, so try to deal with them when freshly done.

On all fabrics: Work some glycerine into the stain, then apply a pad of cottonwool dampened with white vinegar over it. Let it stand for five minutes. Next work a little liquid detergent into the stain with your fingertips, then sponge with cold water. Blot dry. Repeat the treatment as many times as necessary.

Another way is to sponge the stain with methylated or white spirit (dilute the alcohol in 2 parts of water for man-made fibres).

If any traces remain, wipe with hydrogen peroxide (20 vol.). Sponge with water and blot dry.

Water spots and rings
Water spots, rain spots on fabrics such as velvet, felt, taffeta, silk, moiré can be removed by holding the fabric in the steam from a boiling kettle (not too near the spout). Press while damp.

Methylated spirit on a clean cloth dabbed over the mark will also remove water stains. Next dab with a clean soft dry cloth.

On satin: Rub gently with tissue paper in a circular motion.

On french-polished wood: If the mark is slight, rub it with metal polish, then wax and shine.

114

Or rub it with some cigar or cigarette ash mixed to a paste with some salad oil. On light french-polished wood rub the mark with an oily Brazil nut.

Or rub the mark with ammonia then polish.

If water has penetrated the wood, mix equal parts of linseed oil and turpentine and rub into the mark with a soft cloth.

Or rub over the mark with vaseline, coat it and leave overnight. If the next day it is not completely removed, repeat the process.

Watercolour paint
See instructions for *Paint*.

Wax
On all fabrics and carpets: Dab with liquid stain-remover. Next work some liquid detergent into the stain. Rinse and blot dry.

Whisky
See instructions for *Alcoholic beverages*.

Wine
On all washable fabrics: Rinse in warm water, soak in biological detergent solution (follow the packet instructions) or in borax solution (3 tablespoons borax to 1 pint/ $\frac{1}{2}$ litre warm water) or cover the stain with lemon juice and salt for 10 minutes before laundering.

Red wine stains will disappear if white wine is poured over them. Or cover with salt until the wine is absorbed. Afterwards stretch the stained fabric over a container and pour boiling water through the stain, then launder in the usual way.

On linen: Red wine stains will quickly disappear if the stain is dipped in boiling milk while the milk is boiling in a pan over the cooker.

Old stains. Treat white cotton and linen with household chlorine bleach, as directed on bottle, then rinse thoroughly and wash.

Do not use bleach on fabrics with special finishes, i.e., drip-dry. Do not soak coloureds for longer than 15 minutes otherwise slight bleaching may occur.

On non-washable fabrics and upholstery: Blot up as much as possible and sponge with a solution of hydrogen peroxide (20 vol.) (half hydrogen peroxide, half water). Blot dry.

Another way is to blot up as much as possible, then sponge with warm water. Blot well. If any traces remain, sprinkle the stain with talcum powder while still damp. Wait 10 minutes. Brush off. Repeat until clear.

On all carpets: Flush the stain with some soda water from the syphon and blot well. Shampoo. Sponge with cold water. Blot well. Repeat if needed.

Old stains can be loosened up with a glycerine solution (half glycerine, half warm water). Leave it on for half an hour to an hour, then shampoo. Any remaining traces can be removed with methylated spirit or a solution of hydrogen peroxide (20 vol.) (half and half with water).

On leather: First wet the stain with warm water. Next rub it with turpentine. Leave to dry, then polish in the normal way.

Xerox ink
Follow instructions for *Ink* (duplicating ink).

MISCELLANEOUS

Ceramic cooker-tops

To remove stains from a ceramic cooker-top, dab with some hot white vinegar. Leave the vinegar for at least five minutes (more if the top is badly stained) before wiping off.

Ceramic floors

To get rid of shoe marks on a ceramic floor, rub the area with white spirit or turpentine.

Cigarette burns on Bakelite

Burns on Bakelite (plastic) can be removed by rubbing metal polish or paste on the marks.

China

Badly stained coarse china can be cleaned by soaking in neat domestic bleach for a few days. Rinse well.

Earthenware/porous materials

Stains can be removed first by soaking the object in distilled water (from the chemist) until it cannot absorb any more water. Then coat the stains generously with a thick paste made from french chalk and distilled water. After about twenty-four hours, when the paste starts to crack, dust it away. Repeat if necessary. If stains persist, rub them with a piece of cottonwool dipped in methylated spirit or white spirit.

Electrical appliances
Nail-polish remover or liquid lighter fuel will remove plastic which has melted and stuck to electrical appliances. (Do not forget to unplug first.)

Enamel
Stains can be removed by filling the vessel with cold water to which 1 or 2 tablespoons of bleach are added. Leave to stand until the stains disappear and rinse well afterwards. To clean the outside of the pan, use a fine abrasive powder (pumice powder) and a strong detergent. Light stains can be rubbed away with a damp cloth dipped in bicarbonate of soda.

Glass
Burnt stains on glass pans can be removed by soaking pans in cold water to which bicarbonate of soda has been added (2 tablespoons of bicarbonate of soda to 2 pints/1 litre of cold water). Leave to stand for at least an hour. Make sure the inside of the pan is also filled with the solution. See also under *Oven*.

Ivory
To remove marks from ivory, rub on furniture cream and then polish with a clean, soft cloth.

Lacquered trays (Japanese)
Remove heat marks on Japanese lacquered trays by rubbing with vegetable oil until they disappear (the marks, not the trays!).

Leatherette
Man-made leather fabric: A stain can be treated by covering it

122

with a thick paste made from french chalk and water. Leave to dry before brushing off.

See also *Patent leather*.

Lino
Black marks on lino will disappear by simply using a pencil-eraser. Silver polish will also work.

Mackintosh
Do not try to remove a stain on a rubber mackintosh with a grease solvent. Cover the stain with a thick paste made from french chalk and water. Leave to dry before brushing off.

Marble
Yellow stains on white marble can be removed by generously coating with a thick paste made from scouring powder and bleach. Cover with a piece of plastic clingfilm to keep the paste from drying out too quickly. Leave overnight. Remove. The bleach will continue to work on the marble for a little while after the paste has been removed.

Other stains (except grease and oil) on marble should respond to the hydrogen peroxide and ammonia treatment: pour some hydrogen peroxide on to the stain and then sprinkle on a few drops of ammonia. It will bubble slightly. When bubbling has finished, rinse three or four times with cold water.

Onyx
To clean stains on onyx, rub the area with methylated spirit. Onyx being a porous stone, be sure to wipe up any spills immediately and further protect surface with a good wax polish.

Oven
To clean burnt-on food stains inside the oven, cover them with dishwasher powder, then place a wet paper towel over them to retain the moisture. Leave overnight and in the morning the stains will come off with light rubbing.

Stains on glass oven doors will be removed if rubbed with bi-carbonate of soda on a damp cloth.

Parchment
See under *Vellum*.

Patent leather
Marks on patent leather will come off if rubbed with methylated spirit.

Pewter
To remove bad stains, rub with finest steel wool dipped in olive oil. The oil will prevent the wool making scratches on the surface.

Piano
To clean very stained piano keys, make a paste with whiting and hydrogen peroxide (20 vol.). Apply to keys, leave to dry overnight before brushing off paste and polishing.

Porcelain, hard paste, non-porous material
To get rid of stubborn stains, first soak the object in distilled water (from the chemist) for 2 hours. The soaking is to prevent the stains from retreating inwards. Then cover each stain with a small piece of cottonwool dipped in a solution of hydrogen peroxide (20 vol) and $\frac{1}{2}$ a coffee-spoon of ammonia. Leave for about 2 hours. Rinse off and dry. Repeat process if necessary, but allow some time in between to let it dry or it may damage the glaze. See also under *Rust stains*.

Prints
When old prints, engravings or etchings are stained by yellowish spots of rust, they can be cleaned by dipping them in a solution of 2 tablespoons of hydrogen peroxide (20 vol.) to 6 tablespoons of water and a few drops of ammonia. Leave for half an hour and then rinse under running water. Lie the print on blotting-paper to dry. To avoid any wrinkling cover the print with another piece of blotting-paper and some heavy books while drying.

Quarry tiles
To get white patches out of a quarry-tiled floor, brush the tiles with a solution of vinegar (2 teacups) and warm water (4 pints/2 litres). Repeat if necessary.

Rubber mats (bath, sink, etc.)
Stains on bath or sink rubber mats will disappear if rubbed with a soap-filled steel-wool Brillo pad, dipped in bicarbonate of soda.

Shoes
Stains on dark leather shoes will disappear if rubbed with methylated spirit. Stains on light leather shoes will disappear if rubbed with turpentine. Remove stains from brown shoes with a few drops of lemon juice or vinegar mixed with a few drops of water.

Marks on light suede shoes can be removed by rubbing talcum

125

powder into the stains and leaving overnight. Or rub with a clean pencil-eraser.

Stained lizard and skin shoes can be cleaned by dabbing with hydrogen peroxide. Leave to dry and polish with a soft cloth.

See also under *Ceramic floors*.

Steel knives
To remove stains from steel knives, rub with a little scouring powder moistened with lemon juice, or rub on a cork dipped in scouring powder.

Straw
Stains on straw or rush matting can be removed with benzine rubbed over the stain. This process is also good for coloured mats.

Umbrella
When stained, clean with a cloth dipped in vinegar.

Vellum
To clean stains on vellum, rub the spots with a soft cloth dampened with a little benzine.

To remove stains, rub with carbon tetrachlora methane on a soft cloth.

Vinyl floor
Rub black heel marks on vinyl floors with scouring powder on a damp cloth, or silver polish, or toothpaste on a damp cloth, and they will disappear.

Dark marks left by furniture legs on a wooden floor can be removed if rubbed with a damp cloth dipped in paraffin oil.

Index

acetate, 29
acetic acid, 13. *See also* vinegar
acetone, 13
acids, 51
Acrilan, 29
acrylic, 29
adhesive, 51−2. *See also* glue
alcohol, 13−14
alcoholic beverages, 52−3. *See
  also* beer *and* wine
alkalis, 14, 53−4
ammonia, 14
amyl acetate, 14
angora, 30. *See also* mohair
animal glue, 75−6
animal stains, 54
antiperspirants, 54−5
Araldite, *see* adhesive

Bakelite, 121
baking soda, *see* bicarbonate of
  soda
ballpoint, *see* ink
batiste, 30
Beaucaire, 52
beer, 55−6
beeswax, 56
beetroot, 56−7
benzine, 14
berries, 74−5
bicarbonate of soda, 14
bird droppings, 57
blackberry, 74−5
blackcurrant, 74−5
bleach, 15, 25
blood, 57−9
blue, 15
borax, 15
bran, 15; water, 32
brandy, *see* alcoholic beverages
brocade, 30
butter, *see* grease

calico, 30
candle wax, 60−1
candlewick, 30
canvas, 31

car oil, *see* grease
car polish, 61
caramel, 61
carbon paper, 61−2
carrot juice, *see* grass
cashmere, 31
castor oil, 15
cat's puddle, *see* animal stains
ceramics, 121
cheesecloth, 31
chenille, 31
cherry, *see* fruits, fruit juices
chewing gum, 62−3
chiffon, 31
china, 14, 121
chintz, 31−2
chlorine bleach, *see* bleach
chlorine lime, 16
chocolate, 63−4
chrome, 14. *See also* mercuro
  chrome
chutney, 64
cigarettes, *see* nicotine *and* scorch
  marks
Coca-Cola, 64
cocoa, *see* chocolate
cod liver oil, 64−5
coffee, 63−4, 66
colour fastness, 25, 29−46, 49
cooker-tops, ceramic, 121
copper, 21
Copydex, *see* adhesive
corduroy, 32
correction fluid, 66−7
cosmetics, 67
cotton, 32
cough mixture, *see* medicines
Courtelle, 29
crayon, 67−8
cream sauce, 68−9
cream soup, 69
creases, 26
creosote, 69
crêpe and crêpe-de-chine, 32−3
curry, 69−70
cycle oil, *see* grease

Dacron, 41–2
damask, 33
dandelion, see grass
denim, 33
deodorants, 54–5
detergents: enzyme, 16; liquid, 16, 49
Dralon, 29
dry-cleaning, 26, 29–46; fluid, 14
duplicating ink and powder, see ink
dustbins, 16
dye and dyeing, 26; acrylics, 29; colour change, 13, 14; lace, 35; stains, 70–1; testing, 14. See also hair dye

earthenware, 121–2
egg, 71–2
electrical appliances, 122
embroidery transfer, 72
emery cloth, 16
enamel, 122
engine oil, see grease
enzymes, see detergents
epoxy resin, see adhesive
ether, 16
eucalyptus oil, 16
excreta, 54
eye make-up, see cosmetics
eyebrow pencil, 72

fats, see grease
felt, 34
felt-tipped pen, see ink
fish glue, 75–6
fish oil, see cod liver oil
flannel, 34
floors: ceramic, 121; lino, 123; vinyl, 126
flower stains, see grass
fly paper, 72–3
fly stains, 73
foliage, see grass
food colouring, 73
foundation cream, see cosmetics
fountain-pen ink, see ink
french chalk, 16–17
french polish, 73–4
frost, 26
fruit, fruit juices, 74–5
fuller's earth, 17

furniture leg marks, 126
furniture polish, see grease
furring in irons, 27

gaberdine, 34
gilder's white, see whiting
gin, see alcoholic beverages
glass, 14, 17, 18, 122
glue, 75–6. See also adhesive
glycerine, 17
gold lamé, 30
grape, see fruits, fruit juices
grass, 76
gravy, 76
grease, 77–80

hair dye, 80
hair lacquer, 80–1
hair oil, 81
hand cream, 81–2
handkerchiefs, 27
hard paste, 124
hard water, 13. See also softeners
hessian, 34
honey, 82
household bleach, see bleach
hydrogen peroxide, 17

ice cream, 82
ink, 82–8
iodine, 17, 88–9
irons and ironing, 26–7, 29–46
ivory, 18, 122

jam, 89
Japanese lacquered trays, 122
jeans, see denim
jersey, 35
jeweller's rouge, 17
jewellery, 14, 17, 18

kerosene, 18
ketchup, see sauces: bottled
knives, steel, 126

lace, 35–6
lacquer, 90. See also hair lacquer
lacquered trays, Japanese, 122
lamé, 30
lanolin, 18
lead pencil, see pencil

leather: conditioning, 15, 18, 19, 20; marks, 90
leatherette, 122–3
leaves, see grass
linen, 36
lingerie, 34
lino, 123
linseed oil, 18, 90
lipstick, see cosmetics
liquid detergent, see detergents
liquid paraffin, see paraffins
liquors, see alcoholic beverages

machine oil, 91
mackintosh, 123
marble, 123
mascara, see cosmetics
mats, rubber, 125
mayonnaise, 91
meat juices, 91
medicines, 91–2
mercuro chrome, 92–3
metal polish, 93
metal stains, 93
methylated spirit, 18
mildew, 93–6
milk, 96
mirrors, 18
model-making cement, see adhesive
mohair, 36
moiré, 37
mud, 96–8
muslin, 37
mustard, 98

nail varnish, 90, 98–9
net, 37
nicotine, 99–100
non-porous materials, 124
nylon, 29, 37, 41–2

oilcloth, 38
oils, see grease; hair oil; paraffins
ointment, 100
onyx, 123
orange juice, see fruits, fruit juices
organdie, 38
organza, 38
orlon, 29, 38, 41–2
oven, 14, 123–4
oxalic acid, 18

paint: brushes, 21; cleaning, 14; stains, 100–1
paraffins, 19, 77–80
parchment, see vellum
Paris white, see whiting
patent leather, 124
pencil: black and coloured, 101; lead, 90. See also crayon and eyebrow pencil
perfume, 102
peroxide, see hydrogen peroxide
perspiration, 103
petroleum jelly, see Vaseline
pewter, 124
piano, 124
piqué, 38
pitch, see tar
plastic, see Bakelite and electrical appliances
plasticine, 103
plate marks, 38
plums, see fruits, fruit juices
polyester, 38, 41–2
pongee, see silk
poplin, 39
porcelain, 124
porous materials, 121–2
printing ink, see ink
prints, 124
pumice, 19

quarry tiles, 125

rain spots, 104
raspberry, see fruits, fruit juices
rayon, 39
refrigerator, 14
resin, 104
Ribena, see fruits, fruit juices
rottenstone, 19
rouge, see jeweller's rouge
rubber mats, 125
rum, see alcoholic beverages
rust, 105

sackcloth, 34
saddle soap, 19
salad dressing, see grease
sandpaper, 16
satin, 39
sauces, 105–6; bottled, 59–60; cream, 68–9

scent, see perfume
scorch marks, 106–8, 121
scourers, 19
sea-water marks, 108
sealing wax, 108
serge, 39
sewing machine oil, 108
shantung, 39
shellac, 73–4. See also resin
shoes, 125–6; marks, 121; polish, 108–9; stained, 126
silk, 39–41
silver, 17, 21
silver lamé, 30
silver sand, 20
soft drinks, see fruits, fruit juices
softeners: brushes, 21; fabrics, 29–46; water, 14, 21
solvents, 20
soot, 109–10
Spanish white, see whiting
spirits, see alcoholic beverages
sponging, 49–50
stain removal: general, 49–50.
   See also under individual
   entries
steel knives, 126
stove polish, 110
straw, 126
strawberry, see fruits, fruit juices
suede, 41
suntan lotion, see grease
surgical spirit, 20
syrup, see jam and medicines

taffeta, 42
talcum powder, see french chalk
tannin, 66, 96
tar, 110–11
tea, 66. See also chocolate
tea towels, 27. See also towelling
teak oil, 20
terry towelling, see towelling
testing dyes and fabrics, 14, 49
textiles, 28

Tippex, 66–7
tobacco, see nicotine
tomato juice purée, see fruits, fruit juices
towelling, 42
trays, Japanese lacquered, 122
treacle, see jam
turmeric, 112
turpentine, 20
typewriter ribbon, see ink

umbrella, 126
urine, 54, 112–13

varnish, see paint
Vaseline, 20, 113
vegetable stains, see grass
veil, lace, 36
vellum, 126
velvet, 43–4
vinegar, 21
vinyl floors, 126
viscose, 44
Viyella, 44
vodka, see alcoholic beverages
voile, 44
vomit, 54, 113–14

walnut, 114
washing, 28, 29–46
washing blue, see blue
washing soda, 21
water: hard, 13; rings and spots, 114–15. See also softeners
watercolour paint, see paint: water-based
wax, 115
whisky, see alcoholic beverages
white spirit, 21
whiting, 21
wine, 116–17
wool, 44–6

Xerox ink, see ink